"You're a beaut

"I find it hard to belie[ve] someone special in your life." He tried to keep his voice light. "I can't believe that some gallant Frenchman hasn't grabbed you up."

"The lady's not for grabbing," she said. Then she turned and ran down to the shore.

Suddenly it seemed to Miguel that the years had fallen away and he was eighteen again. From out of the past came the memory of how much he had wanted Bree then, and of how unaware she'd been of the way he felt about her.

He remembered, as though it had been yesterday, that night on the beach when he'd kissed her with all the hunger and passion of his eighteen years. He'd wanted Bree then more than he'd ever wanted anything in his life, but as he'd looked at her face, he'd hesitated. She was Bree, and he loved her. If she ever yielded to him, it would be a gift, not stolen but gladly given.

Bree turned and looked at him. "Now I feel like I've come home."

Dear Reader,

Sophisticated but sensitive, savvy yet unabashedly sentimental—that's today's woman, today's romance reader—you! And Silhouette Special Editions are written expressly to reward your quest for substantial, emotionally involving love stories.

So take a leisurely stroll under the cover's lavender arch into a garden of romantic delights. Pick and choose among titles if you must—we hope you'll soon equate all six Special Editions each month with consistently gratifying romantic reading.

Watch for sparkling new stories from your Silhouette favorites—Nora Roberts, Tracy Sinclair, Ginna Gray, Lindsay McKenna, Curtiss Ann Matlock, among others—along with some exciting newcomers to Silhouette, such as Karen Keast and Patricia Coughlin. Be on the lookout, too, for the new Silhouette Classics, a distinctive collection of bestselling Special Editions and Silhouette Intimate Moments now brought back to the stands—two each month—by popular demand.

On behalf of all the authors and editors of Special Editions,
Warmest wishes,

Leslie Kazanjian
Senior Editor

BARBARA FAITH
Say Hello Again

Silhouette Special Edition

Published by Silhouette Books New York

America's Publisher of Contemporary Romance

To Dawn and John Contney, with happy memories
of a high old time in Key Largo.

To Jean Schwan.

And to the real captain of
Straight on Till Morning.

SILHOUETTE BOOKS
300 East 42nd St., New York, N.Y. 10017

ISBN: 0-373-09436-1

First Silhouette Books printing February 1988

America's Publisher of Contemporary Romance

Printed in the U.S.A.

Books by Barbara Faith

Silhouette Intimate Moments

The Promise of Summer #16
Wind Whispers #47
Bedouin Bride #63
Awake to Splendor #101
Islands in Turquoise #124
Tomorrow Is Forever #140
Sing Me a Lovesong #146
Desert Song #173
Kiss of the Dragon #193
Asking for Trouble #208

Silhouette Special Edition

Return to Summer #335
Say Hello Again #436

BARBARA FAITH

is very happily married to an ex-matador whom she met when she lived in Mexico. After a honeymoon spent climbing pyramids in the Yucatán, they settled down in California—but they're vagabonds at heart. They travel at every opportunity, but Barbara always finds the time to write.

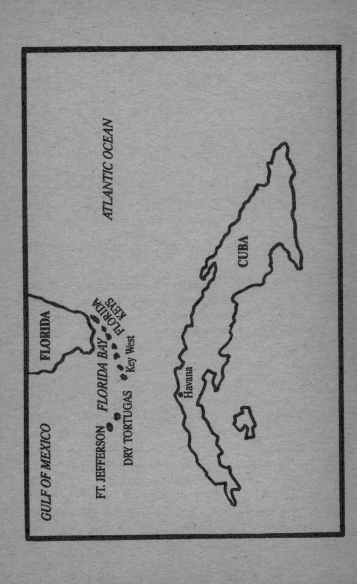

Chapter One

There was something about this particular time of day that never failed to move Miguel Rivas. Whatever the day had been like before—whether the seas had been running strong or calm, whether the trade winds had blown, or not—a stillness came at sunset when the horizon turned into spreading puffs of flamingo and orange and fading pink. Then, just before it darkened, the sky, even the foam-crested waves, turned an incredible shade of gold. And the winds, like the last sigh of a fading sky, diminished to a whisper.

Miguel breathed deeply of the salt air on this fair September evening and looked up as the tall white sails of *Straight On Till Morning* caught the evening breeze. His skin, already tanned by the sun and by the blood of his Spanish and Cuban ancestors, was bronzed by the fading light. With his hand gentle on the tiller he headed his forty-foot yawl toward Key

West. Only once did he look back in the direction of Cuba.

Miguel had been eleven when his family, together with fourteen other people, had set sail from Varadero Beach in a wide, flat-bottomed boat that should have held no more than eight. They had the clothes on their backs and less than one hundred dollars, all that remained after the government expropriated his father's fleet of fishing boats.

The seventeen desperate people made it past the Cuban gunboats to the dubious safety of the open sea. They'd brought enough food and water for the few days it would take to reach the Florida coast—but they hadn't counted on a Caribbean storm.

Nine days passed before the crew of a fishing boat picked them up fifty miles off the southern tip of Florida. By then four of the seventeen had died.

The shadows lengthened as Miguel looked back once again toward the land of his birth, the land he would never see again. His thoughts turned to all that had happened in the past twenty-three years, the way his father had struggled to support the family, and of his own efforts to help.

As soon as he'd been old enough, Miguel had gone to work on the docks, cleaning fish and swabbing decks for the charter-boat captains. He hadn't minded the work, only the jibes from a few of his schoolmates who'd held their noses and wisecracked that he smelled of fish when he passed them in the halls. The wisecracks had stopped the day he flattened Clarence "Bull" Kolwoski, the leader of the group.

After a stint in the navy he'd gone to Florida State, but he'd dropped out after two years and had come back to Key West and gotten a job on a shrimp boat.

Like his father, he'd started with nothing. But he'd worked hard and today he and his father owned the largest fleet of shrimp boats in the Keys. He'd shown them.

Who in the hell were "them" anyway? he wondered now. Guys like Bull Kolwoski, serving out a six-year sentence up in Raiford? Or the girls who'd turned up their delicate noses when he asked them out?

Miguel reached into the pocket of his well-worn jeans and pulled out the invitation that read, "The class of 1972 invites you to attend the fifteenth reunion of Key West High School."

Had it really been fifteen years? At times those years seemed far away, at other times—like tonight—they seemed like only yesterday. Miguel closed his eyes and saw again the world as it had been the spring he turned eighteen.

Every day that term he'd arrived at school early, lingering under the shade of the big banyan tree, scuffing the toes of worn tennis shoes in the dirt, waiting for that first heart-clutching sight of Brianna Petersen.

Bree wasn't like the other girls at Key West High— she was a lady. Her mother insisted she wear either skirts and blouses or high-necked cotton dresses to school and even back then that was the only thing Miguel agreed with her mother about. He liked Bree in dresses; she wouldn't have been the same in the jeans and tight T-shirts the other girls wore.

In the spring of her seventeenth year he'd thought her the most beautiful girl in the world. It had bothered Miguel that socially they were worlds apart, but nothing could have stopped him from dreaming that some day Bree would be his.

Miguel tightened his hand on the tiller and a bitter smile crossed his rugged features. It didn't seem possible that after all these years the thought of Bree Petersen could still jar him. Or that the idea of seeing old schoolmates would make him remember the hurts inflicted because he'd been an outsider, a refugee kid who spoke broken English.

It was because of his English that one of the teachers had asked Bree to tutor him in their sophomore year. Bree—who'd done no more than smile shyly at him in whatever classes they had together—had agreed. The first few sessions had been at Bree's house on Eaton Street. He'd been uncomfortable with the way Cornelia Petersen hovered over them, watching and ready to spring if he so much as touched her daughter's hand.

By mutual consent he and Bree had decided to go to his home to study, Cornelia had protested, but Lars Petersen had, for perhaps the first time in his life, overruled his wife.

The Rivas house wasn't as elegant as the Petersen's. The furniture was what had been available at the Salvation Army rather than antique Georgian, but the kitchen smelled homey and inviting from the freshly baked bread and the black beans that simmered on the stove. He and Bree studied at the round dining-room table to the accompaniment of the beat of rumbas and boleros played on a radio tuned to a Havana station. His mother had taught them to dance, and to this day the only music Miguel felt comfortable dancing to had that insistent Latin beat.

In the warmth of the Rivas home some of Bree's shyness left her. She'd laughed at his father's jokes, listened to his younger sister's problems and watched his mother cook. But most importantly, she and Miguel had become friends and confidants.

He told her things he'd never told anyone else, like the way he felt that dark night when the boat had slipped silently away from the Cuban shore and he'd known he would never return to his homeland.

Even his parents hadn't known how he felt. "Children adjust," Antonio Rivas had said. "Miguel and Lupita were young when we left Cuba, they barely remember the country of their birth."

But Miguel remembered. He remembered Sunday afternoons walking along the *malecon* with his father, the men in their white *guayaberas* drinking *café con leche* in the sidewalk cafés, the street stalls and the pushcarts, the sweet-sour taste of *champloa*. He never spoke of those things, except to Bree.

She'd listened and sympathized, and once when he told her that his mother had fled to freedom with a jar filled with Cuban soil that was to be buried with her when she died, Bree's eyes had filled with tears. She'd touched the side of his face and said, "Oh, Miguel, I'm sorry. I didn't realize how awful it must have been for all of you to leave everything behind, to know you could never go home again."

He'd felt close to her that day, closer than to his own family.

Bree told him little about herself, but he knew that she tiptoed around her mother and that she adored her quiet father. She talked to him mostly about school activities and about her new interest in photography.

Her father had given Bree a camera for her fifteenth birthday and suddenly a whole new world had opened up for her. She spent every penny of her allowance for film and learned to do her own developing. She took hundreds of pictures of him and his family, of the shrimp boats, the wonderful old trees and the sea.

"The sea is alive," she'd told him once. "It's like every wave is another part of its wholeness, its breath. Sometimes it feels peaceful and sometimes it's angry, but the sea is more alive than anything else in the world. It won't ever die, Miguel, it will just go on forever."

She'd picked up a delicate pink shell and continued, "Anne Morrow Lindbergh called seashells a gift from the sea." She held the shell in the palm of her hand, then she'd handed it to him with a shy smile.

He still remembered her expression that day, the way the sun had shone on her face, and the way the wind blew her hair back off her shoulders.

Just as he remembered his own aching desire. He'd wanted her with all the pent-up passion of a teenage boy whose hormones were boiling in a twenty-four-hour-a-day frenzy. But she'd never known that she set him on fire every time she touched his hand, or that it was agony to be with her and not touch her or tell her how he felt.

By Bree's senior year she'd become such a good photographer that she was asked to be on the staff of the yearbook. Craig Logan, who was also senior-class president, was the editor.

Soon Craig was all Bree talked about. Miguel listened to how clever Craig was, how funny, how brilliant. Jealousy, like a tight green ball of bile, boiled inside him. He grew short-tempered and recalcitrant, even with Bree. But she'd been too absorbed in Craig to notice.

A month before their senior prom Miguel asked her to be his date. Bree hedged, and he'd known she was waiting for Craig to ask her. But Craig hadn't, and three days before the dance she told Miguel she'd go with him.

The night of the prom Miguel waited in Bree's living room. When her father said, "Here she is now," he'd looked toward the stairs. For as long as he lived Miguel didn't think he'd ever forget the way Bree had looked that night. She'd worn a simple gown of white ruffled chiffon that clung to her delicately rounded breasts and narrow waist. Her long blond hair had been drawn back off her face and up into a tumble of curls.

She'd been so beautiful that for a moment he'd had to look away. Then, as she came toward him, he'd handed her a cluster of pink camellias and with trembling fingers had pinned them on one shoulder of her dress.

It wasn't until they'd walked into the ballroom of the Beachcomber Hotel that Miguel had felt a clutch of fear. Bree had been so beautiful and he'd been afraid the others would see it—that Craig would see it—and she'd be whisked away.

Craig had seen, of course. He'd looked at Bree and his eyes had been wide with surprise. His gaze followed them as Miguel led Bree out to the dance floor, but it was late in the evening before Craig asked her to dance.

Jealously Miguel watched Craig press Bree closer, then someone had spoken to him and he'd lost sight of the couple. When at last he'd broken away from the boys he'd been talking to, he looked for Bree. When he didn't see her on the dance floor he went looking for her. He found her in a secluded corner of the ball-room with Craig, and as he'd watched Craig had drawn Bree into his arms and kissed her.

Miguel didn't know whether he'd spoken—he didn't think he had—but suddenly Bree looked up. For a brief moment they stared at each other, then Miguel turned away.

He said little during the rest of the dance or at the after-prom party. He still hadn't spoken when the party broke up and it was time to take Bree home. Several times she'd tried to speak to him, but when he offered no response she moved farther over to her side of his father's old pickup and cast worried glances his way.

She didn't try again until he drove down to a remote section of the beach. In the distance they heard the threatening roll of thunder.

"It's going to rain," Bree said when Miguel stopped the car and turned off the motor.

With a swift motion he pushed her back against the door. He put his arms around her and kissed her with all the pent-up passion in his eighteen-year-old body.

Bree struggled to get away from him, and somehow she had. She'd opened the door and gone running up the beach, and he'd followed. When he caught her he'd pulled her into his arms and kissed her again, as angry and as frustrated as he'd ever been in his life because it wasn't him Bree wanted, it was Craig.

He cupped her face with his hands, holding her while he kissed her. He didn't listen to her gasps of protest or see the flash of lightning that split a jagged edge against the sky because his body had been on fire. He pressed her closer. One single thought had been in his mind, the thought of taking her there on the beach she loved so much.

Miguel dropped to his knees, forcing Bree down to the sand with him. Almost wild with desire, he'd kissed her again and again while she struggled against him. Then, suddenly, Bree's lips had softened and parted under his and she'd held him close as they knelt together.

He'd eased her away from him and looked at her. Her eyes were luminous in the moonlight. Tendrils of her golden hair, mussed by his roughness and by the rising wind, curled softly around her face. He'd looked down at her and the breath had caught in his throat.

He kissed her again, more gently this time. Her lips had trembled against his and her body had been warm and yielding. A moment passed. They looked at each other and a sigh shuddered through Miguel's body. He relaxed his hold and got to his feet. "It's time to go," he said in a voice made rough by emotion.

They didn't speak on the way to her home. Miguel parked and went around the car to help Bree out. He walked her to her door but he didn't kiss her. He only wished her a quiet good-night and without a backward look ran down the walk to the pickup.

Miguel hadn't seen or heard from Bree in fifteen years. From time to time someone spoke about her. He knew that she was living in Paris, making a name for herself taking photographs for *Our World Magazine*.

Miguel thought about her once in a while, and about that night on the beach when he'd come so close to making love to her. But he'd always been able to put the thought of Bree away, somewhere deep in the back of his mind.

Until last week, when Dawn Wintzer had told him that Bree was coming home to Key West for the reunion.

"I've asked her to serve on the alumni committee," Dawn had said. "She'll be here sometime on Sunday."

Today was Saturday.

Darkness closed in around Miguel and in the distance he could see the lights of Key West. He felt the splash of salt spray on his face as a fresh breeze curled the sails of the boat as though to hurry him to shore.

Miguel told himself he didn't care whether he saw Bree Petersen or not. There'd been other women in his life since his schoolboy crush on her. But from time to time the memory of Bree and that night on the beach returned to him like an unwelcome ghost of the past.

Perhaps, he thought now, the time had come to put away the memories that haunted him.

Just before she started over the seven-mile bridge, Bree turned the air conditioner off and rolled down the windows of the rented car. This was a perfect September day, the time of year she loved the best, when the scorching heat of summer lessened and gave way to the perfect balmy weather that made the Keys a haven for the snowbirds from the north.

She'd almost forgotten the technicolor beauty of this long stretch of highway between Miami and Key West. The sky was bluer here, the clouds softer and whiter than anywhere else on earth she'd ever been. The Atlantic on her left and the Gulf of Mexico on her right ran in unbelievable shades of blue, sea green and turquoise, changing as the tides moved. The air, soft with the promise of autumn, held the tang of the sea. She breathed it in and knew that she was almost home.

Home was the old Victorian house on Eaton Street where she'd been born. In her mind's eye Bree could see the feather palms that grew close to the wide front porch, the tall white columns, the fancy gingerbread trim on the upper and lower front porches, the small attic with the dormer window where she'd sat and dreamed of all the things she would do when she was old enough to leave.

A faint smile turned up the corners of Bree's mouth. One of her dreams had been that she would go to New York and become a famous photographer and that one day Craig Logan would see her photographs in *Time* or *Newsweek* or *National Geographic*. He'd come to wherever she was, to Hong Kong, Vienna or Rome, and he'd tell her that he loved her, just as she'd loved him all through her painful high-school years.

Bree flexed her tired shoulders. Part of her dream had come true. She'd become a photographer— though not a famous one—and she'd traveled to all the places she'd dreamed about so long ago. But it hadn't been easy.

She liked working for *Our World Magazine* and she liked living in Paris. But this year she'd become restless and there had been times, right in the middle of an assignment, when she'd found herself dreaming of home.

A month ago Bree had received Dawn's letter and the invitation to the fifteenth-year class reunion.

"We're having it the same place we had the prom, at the Beachcomber," Dawn had written. "You've been away too long, Bree, it's high time you came home."

A week later Dawn had followed up her letter with a phone call and Bree had agreed to return.

Now she was almost there. She passed Bahia Honda, Big Pine and Saddlebunch keys; soon she'd be home.

With a sigh Bree pushed back the hair that blew about her face, a little sad because everything looked so different. The scattered fishing camps all along the highway from Miami had been replaced by new houses, condominiums, restaurants and stores.

Key West would have changed, too, and so would her friends from Key West High School's class of '72.

Bree thought of the four years she'd spent there and wondered who it was who'd said that high-school days were the happiest in a person's life. They hadn't been for her. The years between fourteen and seventeen had probably been her most frustrating, yearning, uncertain years.

She'd been taller than most of the boys in her class, too thin, too gangly and awkward. She'd envied Bobbie Lee Dillon because Bobbie's breasts were a size thirty-six while her own were the size of kumquats, and because Bobbie Lee was so short and cute—two things Bree would have given her life to have been in those years.

It was only after she'd left home and started modeling that she realized that her own attributes weren't so bad, and that five-foot-eight wasn't even considered tall in the world of modeling.

Bree hadn't liked being a model, even though it had eventually led to her becoming the professional photographer she'd always wanted to be. In her modeling years she'd had to pare her weight down to a hundred and fifteen pounds and cut her pale hair in a French bob. As soon as she stopped modeling she'd put on ten pounds and let her hair grow to the shoulder length it was now.

She'd worn it up the night of the prom, Bree suddenly remembered, but it had come down when Miguel kissed her. She smiled. She hadn't thought about Miguel Rivas in a long time and she hadn't seen or heard from him in fifteen years.

Bree wondered what kind of a man he'd turned out to be as she passed the sign that welcomed her to Key West.

Chapter Two

Y ou're too thin." Cornelia Petersen touched the corners of her mouth with the starched linen napkin, then passed the mashed potatoes to Bree.

"I've polished off the salad, a roll and two pork chops. If I eat another helping of mashed potatoes I'm going to burst." Bree smiled and said reassuringly, "It was a delicious dinner, Mother, but I really can't eat another thing."

"It's all that French food." Cornelia sniffed. "All those fancy sauces with fancy names. It's spoiled you for decent home cooking."

Bree looked across the table at her mother and knew it wouldn't do her any good to argue. Cornelia hadn't changed; Cornelia would never change.

Now in her early fifties, and a widow for some time, Bree's mother was a striking, if severe-looking woman. Her back was ramrod straight, her face unlined. The chestnut-brown hair that she still wore pulled back into a tight bun had only the faintest traces of gray. Her figure was the same as it had been thirty years ago, neat and trim and spare.

"How's everything down at city council?" Bree asked, barely stifling a groan as Cornelia placed a large piece of key lime pie in front of her.

"Middling fair. We're still fighting the battle of the high-rises, trying to keep our beaches from being destroyed like Miami's were in the fifties and sixties. That issue is the only thing that dreadful Rivas man and I have ever agreed on."

Bree took a bite of her pie. "Antonio Rivas?"

Cornelia nodded and with a sigh said, "I felt sure he'd be defeated when the last election came around but I suppose every Cuban in Key West voted for him."

"He never remarried after Mrs. Rivas died?"

"No, but the way I hear it he doesn't lack for female company. Probably thinks he's the Don Juan of the Keys." Cornelia glared across the table at Bree. "You'd think a man his age would behave himself."

"His age? He can't be much older then you are, Mother."

"But I act my age."

Bree looked at her mother, wondering if Cornelia had ever acted her age. As long as Bree could remember, her mother had been the staid, middle-aged lady she was today. Changing the subject, Bree said, "How're Lupita and Miguel?"

"Doing very well for themselves. Lupita got herself a degree in accounting at the University of Miami and I guess you know that Miguel owns most of the shrimp boats in Key West. He went to Florida State but he had to drop out when his mother died. He got a job working on old Ben Cooper's boat and when Ben started ailing, Miguel bought the boat from him. From then on seems like it was just one boat after the other. Then he started buying up some of the old houses on Fleming and Olivia. He fixed them up in his spare time, advertised in some of the Northern newspapers and sold 'em to snowbirds for four or five times what he'd paid. He's done well for himself and his family. He owns some office buildings and a big house on the beach where he lives all by himself.''

"He never married?''

Cornelia shook her head. "He's been too busy making money to think about taking a wife. I hear tell he's had his pick of women, though. Likely a Don Juan—just like his father.'' Cornelia pushed back her chair. "Would you like another piece of pie? Here, let me give you just a small—''

The ringing of the telephone interrupted Cornelia. She hurried away and when she came back said, "It's Dawn. She wants to talk to you.''

"Thank you, Mother. But no thanks on the pie.'' Bree hurried into the living room before Cornelia could object.

Dawn sounded cheerful when Bree picked up the phone. "Hi, I see you made it. Everything all right? How's your mother?''

"Fine, although she's determined to fatten me up. When am I going to see you?''

"Tomorrow night for dinner, here at six-thirty. I'll bring you up to date then on what we're doing for the reunion. You and Carris Nelson have been elected official greeters at the reception. We'll talk about it when you get here.''

"Official greeter? I've been away too long, Dawn. I won't know anybody."

"Of course you will. Anyway, you're our most famous alumnus—world traveler, ace photographer, raving beauty."

"Sure, sure. Listen, Dawn, I—"

"It'll be fun, Bree. We'll talk about it tomorrow night. Gwen and Paul are coming. They've got a couple of kids now—a boy and a girl who're holy terrors. I've asked Miguel Rivas, too. You remember him, don't you?" Before Bree could answer, Dawn said, "John's yelling for the phone. See you tomorrow."

"But—" Bree stared at the phone as Dawn clicked off. Her face was thoughtful. Miguel Rivas. She rolled his name around in her mind and wondered what it would be like to see him after all these years.

With the thought of him—of the young man who'd brought her pink camellias on prom night—Bree smiled softly. Miguel had kissed her down on the beach with all the fury of the approaching storm, as angry as the waves that pounded the shore.

Craig Logan had kissed her, too. Bree had had a crush on Craig ever since tenth grade, and when he'd kissed her she'd trembled with excitement. But his kiss had left her unmoved.

Miguel had been different. His kisses had been hard and so fiercely urgent that at first she'd been afraid of him. Then her fear had given way to a feeling she'd never before experienced. She'd parted her lips under his and her body had swayed against him. And she'd trembled with a need she didn't understand.

Fifteen years had passed. There'd been a few men in Bree's life but none of them had affected her the way Miguel Rivas had that windswept night on the beach.

With a sigh and a mental shrug Bree turned away from the phone. All girls remember their first kiss, she told herself. But she wasn't a girl any longer, she was a woman, and Miguel Rivas was a man. It would be pleasant—yes, that was the word—it would be *pleasant* to see him again.

But as Bree went into the kitchen to help her mother with the dishes, she began to plan what she would wear the following night.

Bree chose a summer dress in a delicate shade of peach. With it she wore a shell necklace and earrings and high-heeled white sandals. She debated on whether or not to put her hair up but finally decided to do it in a French braid. Just before she left the house she noticed a bowl of pink camellias on the coffee table and with a wry smile of remembrance took one and tucked it into her hair.

Because it was a balmy evening, Bree decided to walk the ten blocks to Dawn's rather than drive. The streets were quiet and she walked slowly, enjoying the old gingerbread houses and the familiar trees—the gumbo limbos, West Indian almonds and the big Spanish laurel in front of the Old Stone Church.

Bree paused there, remembering hot Sunday mornings when she'd sat between her mother and father. Too warm in her starched cotton dress, she had tapped the toes of her white Mary Janes impatiently until her mother stilled her restlessness with a stern look. She remembered, too, with a touch of bittersweet sadness, her father's comforting hand on hers, and his gentle smile that quieted her until church was over.

Bree slowed her steps as she neared the house where Dawn and John had lived since their marriage. She and Dawn had stayed in touch and Dawn had visited her in both New York and Paris. But Bree hadn't seen Miguel, Gwen or Paul in a long time. She remembered that Paul had been a star quarterback and that Gwen had barely spoken to her all through high school.

The old white house had recently been painted. The shutters were as bright a green as the leafy vines that embraced the front-porch pillars. Bougainvillea, scarlet hibiscus and multicolored crotons grew close to the house. Tall palms lined the walkway.

From inside Bree heard the sound of laughter. She hesitated, one hand on the gate, reluctant for a moment to enter. She'd been away for such a long time. She was no longer a part of this life, or of the people who lived here.

Suddenly the screen door opened and Dawn ran down the steps and threw her arms around Bree. "Where have you been?" she cried. "I couldn't wait for you to get here. I've been jumping up every five minutes to look out the window. How does it feel to be back?" She turned her friend around appreciatively. "You look sensational, Bree."

"So do you. You haven't changed a bit, Dawn," she said with a grin. "You're still wearing the same old ponytail."

Dawn laughed and looped her arm through Bree's. "Come on, everybody's dying to see you." Before Bree could hold back, Dawn rushed her up the stairs and into the house where John, big and blond and as lovable as Bree remembered, gave her a bear hug and welcomed her.

Paul shook hands with her, and Gwen—elegantly dressed in tailored pants and a gray silk blouse—said, "How nice to see you again," in a way that told Bree it wasn't nice at all.

Miguel stood up. "Hello, Bree. Welcome home."

He remained where he was, making no move to either kiss her or take her hand.

John led her to a flowered chintz chair. "What would you like to drink? We're having gin and tonics."

"That would be fine."

She was nervous, Miguel thought as he watched her. She sat quietly, a slight smile touching her lovely mouth, her pale hands folded together in her lap. She would be thirty-three now, a year younger than he was, and while a part of him longed for the seventeen-year-old she'd been, he felt a rush of excitement at the beauty she'd become. She also had a figure that would make any man stop and take stock and speculate. He thought that if he tried, he could span her waist with his two hands, and he found himself wondering what it would feel like to try. Her skin was pale and there were faint smudges of fatigue under her eyes.

"So how do you like living in Paris?" Paul asked. "Key West must seem like pretty small potatoes to you now."

Bree shook her head. "No, it's good to be home."

"I'm surprised you're still single, Bree dear. I'd have thought you would have had dozens of Frenchmen asking you out." Gwen raised one delicate eyebrow. "But you never did date very much, did you? Even in high school."

"No, I don't suppose I did." Bree took a sip of her drink.

"I never saw you at any of the dances, but maybe that was because you were taller than most of the boys." Gwen's glance slid to Miguel. "Except for Miguel and Craig Logan. You remember Craig, don't you?"

"Of course." Bree turned to Dawn and tried to change the subject. "What kind of a band are we going to have for the dance Saturday night?"

"A new group. They were at the Americana in Miami last season and—"

"You had a terrible crush on him," Gwen interrupted. She looked at the others and with a laugh said, "Poor Bree, she'd get absolutely tongue-tied every time Craig walked into a room. He pawned off most of the work on the yearbook on to her and she did it gladly. She worshiped him."

"Worship isn't exactly the word," Bree said carefully.

"We all had crushes when we were seventeen," Dawn said. "Bree wasn't any different than we were."

"But we always got the boys we went after." Gwen smiled over the rim of her glass. "Bree didn't."

"Then now's her chance," John said. "You knew that Craig married Bobbie Lee, didn't you, Bree?"

She nodded. "They got married the same year I went to Paris, didn't they?"

"Yep." John drained his glass. "But it's been rocky. Bobbie Lee lost a baby a couple of years ago. When she found out she couldn't have children she started drinking."

"And Craig started running around with some gal from Plantation Key," Paul said. "He and Bobbie Lee split and she stayed on in the home they'd bought a couple of years ago and Craig rented a condo on the beach.''

"Yeah." John reached for a piece of cheese. "And every single woman between nineteen and fifty-nine has been circling overhead. Old Craig's still got it, I guess.''

Paul grinned at Bree and in a lazy drawl he said, ''I reckon you came back at just the right time, sugar.''

Bree looked down at her drink and wished with every bone in her body that she'd never left Paris. If this was what coming home meant and if these were the friends she'd left behind, she'd be wise to take the first plane back to Paris.

When Dawn stepped in to change the subject Bree looked up and saw Miguel watching her, his dark eyes wryly amused.

Bree looked at him, trying to see something of the boy she'd known in the man who faced her now. He'd been a handsome boy and he'd grown to be a handsome man. But there was a cynicism about his dark good looks that hadn't been there before, a hint of danger in his eyes that disquieted her. His body was lean and hard and muscular; the hand that held his glass looked powerful and strong.

Dawn seated Miguel next to Bree at dinner, and though he spoke little, Bree was very aware of him beside her. Once when she reached for her wineglass her hand brushed his and it was as though a current of electricity ran through her. He turned to look at her, his gaze intense as it rested first on her eyes, then on her lips.

After dinner the talk turned to plans for the reunion.

"The reception will be on Tuesday night," Dawn said. "Then we'll have the beach party Wednesday afternoon and a free day Thursday. Friday night's the banquet and the dance will be Saturday night—out on the terrace overlooking the water if the weather's nice, in the ballroom if it isn't."

"It said on the noon news that a hurricane's brewing somewhere off Puerto Rico," Paul said.

"There's always a hurricane brewing somewhere this time of year." Dawn scribbled a note on the yellow pad on her lap. "Somebody remind me to double-check with the hotel about the food for the beach party. And I've got to call the band to make sure they're going to play some of the songs from 1972."

The talk went on during coffee and dessert. When at last the evening drew to a close Bree said goodnight, and promising to call Dawn the next day, turned to leave.

"Where's your car?" Miguel asked as she started down the steps.

"I walked. It isn't too far."

"But it's late." Miguel took her arm. "Come on, I'll drive you home." Seeing her hesitation he said, "Things have changed since you've been away, Bree, not just in Key West but all over the world. You really shouldn't be out alone this late." Before she could argue he opened the car door and helped her inside. "Have you been down to the beach yet?" he asked.

Bree shook her head. "I drove in from the Miami airport yesterday afternoon. Jet lag always bothers me so I slept in this morning." She rolled down the window and looked out at the old houses. "Nothing seems to change, does it?"

"I guess you haven't seen Mallory Square or walked down Duval Street yet. Everywhere you go it's knee-deep in people. I guess I like Key West the way it was, or maybe I'm just jealous of all those snowbirds discovering my town."

His town? Was that the way he thought of it now? Bree glanced at him, wondering if he'd ever felt the need to return to the country of his birth.

"Have you ever been back?" she asked. "To Cuba, I mean?"

"No." Miguel switched the radio on and the Latin music that she hadn't heard in years filled the car as he headed toward the beach. "This is my home. I'll never go back—none of us will."

He parked and when he turned to her Bree said, "I'm sorry about your mother, Miguel." She wondered if they'd buried the jar of Cuban soil with Alicia Rivas as she'd asked. She hoped they had.

"We got your flowers," Miguel said. "Thanks." He leaned his head back against the seat of the car for a moment. Then abruptly he sat up and opened the door. "Let's walk a bit, shall we?"

The scent of the sea was strong, and for a moment, nostalgia, sweet and sad and painful, assailed her. This is the real coming home, she thought, not the house on Eaton Street or friends like Gwen, but this quiet night, the smell of the sea and the sound of the waves rolling in to the shore.

She took her sandals off and felt the cool sand under her feet. She smiled up at Miguel when he came around the car and took her hand.

"*Did* you have dozens of Frenchmen asking you out?" he asked

"Of course!" Bree laughed and with a shake of her head said, "I haven't changed all that much, Miguel, I've just gotten older. Gwen's right. I didn't date much in high school and I don't date all that much now. I travel a lot and I'm awfully busy with my job."

"Too busy for a serious relationship?" He stopped and looking at her said, "You're a beautiful woman, Bree. I find it hard to believe that there isn't someone special in your life." He tried to keep his voice light. "I can't believe that some gallant Frenchman hasn't grabbed you up."

"The lady's not for grabbing," she said. Then she turned and ran down to the shore.

Miguel watched her. As she drew closer to the water she lifted her dress to her knees and stepped into the waves. The night was clear and in the golden light of a slice of new moon the fine slender lines of her body and the long shapeliness of her legs were outlined.

Suddenly it seemed to Miguel that the years had fallen away. He was eighteen again and Bree was his girl. From out of the past came the memory of how much he'd wanted her and of how unaware she'd been of the way he'd felt.

He remembered that night on the beach when he'd kissed her with all the hunger and passion of his eighteen years as though it had been yesterday. They'd knelt on the sand, their bodies close, and he'd kissed her until her lips had softened under his and she'd wrapped her arms around his neck.

When they parted he'd gazed at her lovingly. Her eyes had been luminous and her hair had loosened to fall softly around her face. Even now, he remembered the roll of thunder in the distance and the threatening growl of the waves against the shore.

He'd wanted Bree more than he'd ever wanted anything in his life, but as he'd looked at her face, illuminated by a sudden slash of lightning, he'd hesitated, held back by a feeling that was bigger than the terrible urgency that burned through his body. He loved her. If she ever yielded to him it would be a gift, not stolen, but gladly given.

Bree turned and looked at him. The moonlight touched her hair. "It's wonderful," she called out over the sound of the waves.

Miguel went down the sand toward her and when she turned away from the water and moved toward him she said, "Now I feel like I've come home. Thank you for bringing me here, Miguel."

He wanted to touch her. He wanted to pull her into his arms and pretend he was eighteen years old again. "It's late. I'd better get you home," he said gruffly. Not trusting himself to touch her, he turned and started back to the car.

At the car he knelt down to help her brush the sand off her bare feet. Her skin was cool against his fingers. He circled her ankle with his thumb and first finger and felt her grow still.

"You're too thin," he said, and his voice sounded harsh in the quietness of the night.

"That's . . . that's what my mother says." She took a deep breath.

"She's right. And you're too pale. You need some sun." He had to make himself let go of her. When he stood up he said, "How long will you be staying, Bree?"

"I'm not sure. I have a two-week vacation but I'm tired. I may stay a little longer than that."

"So there really isn't anybody to rush back to?"

Bree looked at him, then away. "No," she said softly.

They spoke little on the way to her house. When he stopped the car he came around to her door to walk her to the steps. "It was nice to see you again, Bree," he said.

The silence hung between them after they said their good-nights.

After Bree went inside and closed the door Miguel stood for a moment looking up at the house. Then he went back down the walk to the car and in the glow from the porch he saw the pink camellia that had fallen from her hair.

Chapter Three

Bree had expected Miguel to call, but four days passed and he didn't. On the Monday before the reunion, Bree drove down to the docks with Dawn.

"How many shrimp do you think a hundred and eighty people will eat?" Dawn asked.

"For cocktails or appetizers?"

"Appetizers."

"Five or six?"

"Let's make it ten." Dawn slammed the door of her ancient but still classy MG and headed for the pier. "I called Antonio Rivas. He's getting the shrimp for us. You remember him, don't you?"

"Of course. I've always liked him."

"Your mother doesn't." Dawn grinned at her. "She's been gunning for him for years. Is it because he's Cuban?"

Bree shook her head. "Mother's not prejudiced but she's like a lot of the old-time Conchs—if you haven't been born and bred right here in Key West you're an outsider."

"It's kind of funny the way the two of them never agree. Every time a new issue comes up before the city council we all know what's going to happen. Antonio's a darling man but he can be just as stubborn as your mother." Dawn looked away from Bree and waved. "There he is now. Come on."

Antonio Rivas was a fine-looking man in his mid-fifties. He was a head shorter than Miguel and a good twenty-five pounds heavier. He had a thick head of curly black hair threaded with silver at his temples, a big black mustache, wide shoulders and a barrel chest matted with a thatch of black hair that was visible through the opening of his half-buttoned shirt.

He called out when he spotted the two women, then he hurried forward to shake Dawn's hand and to hug Bree. "Just look at you," he said when he held her away from him. "You're the prettiest thing I've seen in a long time. Are you home for good or have you only come back for the reunion?"

"For the reunion and a vacation," Bree said as she smiled at him.

"You're a big time photographer now, aren't you? And *por Dios*, you're good. Very good."

"You've seen some of my photographs?"

"I've seen them all. Miguel has a stack of magazines a mile high with your pictures in them. He even has copies of all those photos you took when you were just beginning, back when you were in school. You've come a long way, *muchacha*. The pictures you took of the street people in London last winter during the cold spell almost made me cry. You've got a way with your camera that seems to look right into the heart of people."

Bree looked at Antonio, surprised that anyone except her mother had kept track of her work. She was amazed that Miguel had followed her career, and touched because he'd kept copies of photos she'd given him when she was still in high school.

"I've got those shrimp you ordered, Mrs. Wintzer," Antonio told Dawn. "They're all packed in ice. I figured nine or ten apiece ought to do it, but if you want more there won't be any problem."

"No, Mr. Rivas, that sounds fine to me."

"Then come on in the office and let's have a cup of coffee." He draped his arm over Bree's shoulder. "Bet you haven't had any good Cuban coffee in a long time. Maybe you've been spoiled by the coffee they serve in France. I bet a good cup of Cuban coffee would knock you right on your ear."

"I bet it wouldn't." Bree smiled at him. "Do you have any *churros*?"

"Of course I do. I knew you were coming, didn't I? Lupita baked them first thing this morning."

As soon as they entered Antonio's office Bree smelled the steaming aroma of the Cuban coffee she hadn't tasted in almost fifteen years. Antonio poured it and handed a demitasse to both Bree and Dawn. The flavor was as strong and as good as she remembered. She took a bite of the *churro*—the skinny pastry that's a cross between a fritter and a doughnut—and licked the sugar off her fingertips. "Now I know I've really come home. This is wonderful, Antonio. Please thank Lupita."

"Thank her yourself tonight." Antonio turned to Dawn. "We want you and your husband and Bree to have dinner with us this evening. Lupita stayed home to cook *arroz con pollo* and *frijoles negros* for Bree. And I've got a bottle of dark Jamaican rum I've been saving for a special occasion. Tonight we'll—" He hesitated as Miguel stepped into the office.

"Tonight we'll what?" Miguel asked. "Hello, Dawn—Bree." He looked at her, then quickly turned his glance back to his father.

"We'll drink some rum and eat *arroz con pollo* to celebrate Bree's coming home. I've invited her for dinner, along with Mrs. Wintzer and her husband."

"Oh?" One dark brow shot up. "What time?"

"Seven o'clock. Is that okay with the two of you?"

"I can't," Dawn said. "I'm sorry, but I've got to go to a company dinner with John."

"Then we'll do it another night while Bree's here. But from Bree I refuse to take no for an answer."

She looked up at Miguel. His face was impassive. He wore a black and white checked shirt that was open at the throat and well-worn blue jeans. "I... I don't want to impose," she said, pulling her gaze away from Miguel.

"Impose! What impose? It's nice weather, we'll eat outside and listen to some good Latin music. All right?"

Bree nodded. "All right, Antonio. Thank you. I'd love to come." She didn't look at Miguel.

"Ask your mother, too."

Bree hesitated, then truthfully said, "I think she's got a meeting of the historical society tonight."

"Okay." Antonio ran a hand across his chin. "But a week from Saturday we're having a big family reunion at our house. You and your mother are both invited and you tell her I won't take no for an answer from her either.''

"Saturday night is the night of the dance at the Beachcomber,'' Miguel told his father. "Bree and I will both be there, Dad. I'm sorry, I wish you'd made the family get together on a different day.''

"So am I.'' Antonio looked upset, then said with a shrug, "But you can come before the dance, and maybe after. When the family gets together and everybody starts talking, a party could go on all night.'' He looked at Bree. "What time does your dance begin?''

"Nine o'clock,'' Bree said.

"Then you and Miguel come at five-thirty—and bring your mother. You and Miguel can leave whenever you want to. If Cornelia wants to stay I'll take her home later.''

"Fine,'' Bree said with a smile, knowing very well it would take every bit of her persuasive powers to get her mother to go. And if Cornelia *did* agree to go she certainly wouldn't allow Antonio Rivas to take her home.

"Are you going to check into the Beachcomber during the reunion?'' Miguel asked Bree.

"Yes, I might as well be where the action is, especially since I'm on the committee. Are you going to stay there?''

"Uh-huh.'' He eased himself away from the desk he'd been leaning against. "I'll pick you up at six-thirty tonight if that's okay''

"Yes, that'll be fine.''

"Good. I'll see you then. So long, Dawn.'' To his father he said, "I'll be on the *Sweet Sue* if you want me." But still Miguel hesitated. For another moment his gaze rested on Bree. Then, as though physically pulling himself away, he crossed the room and went out the door.

He had mixed feelings about seeing her tonight, about seeing her at all for that matter, and he wished his father hadn't asked her to dinner. It wasn't that he didn't like Bree or that he didn't find her attractive. He did. She was a beautiful woman, but because there were so many memories involved, she was a dangerous one to him. He'd loved her when he was eighteen and loving Bree had hurt like hell. He wasn't about to go through that again.

But God! Every time he looked at her he wanted to touch her. He knew, deep in his bones, that if he saw too much of her he just might fall in love with her again, and he had no intention of doing that. His life was here in Key West, hers was in Paris, or London, or Rome—wherever her magazine sent her.

Besides, he thought as he headed for the trawler, he and Bree were from different worlds, at least as far as her mother was concerned.

Miguel still remembered Cornelia Petersen's antipathy toward the Rivas family. She was a strong, opinionated woman, and some of the things she felt would have had to have rubbed off on her daughter. Besides, Bree had made it clear when she was seventeen that there was a fine line between friendship and romantic involvement.

That was fifteen years ago, a voice in his head whispered. She was only going to be here for a couple of weeks and they would be thrown together because of the reunion. Why couldn't he relax and let himself enjoy being with her? Just because they would spend time together, didn't mean they would have to become involved.

But he was jumping the gun, he told himself. He'd forgotten about Craig Logan and that in another few months Craig would be a free man. A frown crossed Miguel's face. Was Craig the real reason Bree had returned to Key West? Had she known that Craig and Bobbie Lee were divorcing? Had she come home hoping to see Craig, to try to recapture the dream she'd had so long ago?

A frown drew Miguel's brows together as he looked up at the *Sweet Sue* and called a greeting to her captain. The afternoon crept by. He snapped orders at workmen he'd never snapped at before. He bawled out the captain, then apologized, and wondered what the hell was wrong with him.

What was wrong, he knew, was that in another few hours he'd see Bree again, and he wasn't sure how he felt about that.

"I swear to goodness I don't know why you're going over there," Cornelia said as she watched Bree dress. "You're only going to be here for two weeks, I thought we'd spend more time together."

"You were invited, too, mother."

"Humph!" A frown puckered Cornelia's smooth forehead. "As if I'd ever set foot in that man's house."

"We're both invited for a family get-together next Saturday." Bree studied herself in the mirror, wondering whether to braid her hair or leave it as it was, soft and slightly curling around her shoulders. Deciding to leave it loose, she turned to her mother and said, "I'm going and I think you should, too."

"But—"

"I'll only be here for a little while, Mother. I'll very likely be seeing Miguel and it would mean a lot to me if you'd try to get along with both him and his father."

"By seeing, do you mean dating?"

"No," Bree said, a little too quickly. "I . . . I meant because of the reunion."

"He's picking you up tonight."

"Only because his father invited me." They heard a car stop in front of the house and a door slam. Bree took a deep breath and looked at herself in the mirror. "Do I look all right?" she asked her mother.

Cornelia nodded. With a softening of expression she said, "You've turned into a beautiful woman, Bree. That shade of blue is perfect for you." Then with a touch of asperity she added, "But I can't say I approve of that neckline."

Bree laughed and hugged her mother. "Will you let Miguel in, please? Tell him I'll be right down."

She turned to look in the mirror when Cornelia left the room, wondering if her mother had been right about the neckline that showed the slight rise of her breasts. She fastened a string of pearls around her throat and matching earrings to her ears. Then with a smile she went out to meet Miguel.

He was waiting for her at the bottom of the stairs, and suddenly, looking down at him, the memory of prom night came back to Bree. She hadn't wanted to go to the prom with Miguel, but Craig Logan hadn't asked her. When she'd seen Miguel standing at the bottom of the stairs she'd paused, though, and a feeling she'd never experienced before swept through her. He'd looked suddenly very grown up in his white jacket and dark trousers, very masculine and handsome.

She'd been glad then that it was Miguel who'd asked her to the prom and her heart had begun to beat hard and her breath had caught in her throat. He'd looked up at her and for a moment she hadn't been able to breathe.

Now as she descended the stairs he looked up, and unexpectedly, ridiculously, Bree felt the same as she had fifteen years ago. I'm not seventeen, she tried to tell herself, but the remembered excitement was there and the hand she held out to greet Miguel trembled.

If he noticed he didn't speak of it. His hand was cool when he took her arm.

She kissed her mother's cheek and let Miguel lead her out the door.

The old house on Windsor Lane had been painted. The flowers and shrubs that Mrs. Rivas had planted years ago still flourished. As Miguel opened the car door Bree could hear the beat of Latin music emanating from the house. The screen door banged and Lupita ran down the front steps to meet her.

"*Bienvenida,*" Lupita said as she took Bree's hand. "My goodness, Bree, you look so beautiful!"

"So do you," Bree said with a laugh as she looked at Lupita. At twenty-seven Lupita Rivas had come into her own as a woman. She was almost as tall as Miguel, with a floating cloud of heavy black hair, big dark eyes fringed with long lashes, a slender nose and sweetly full lips. She wore an apron tied around the waist of her yellow summer dress.

"It's wonderful to see you again," Bree said. "Thanks for the *churros*, they were delicious." She put her arm around Lupita's waist. "Whatever you're cooking smells wonderful."

"*Arroz con pollo*," Lupita said. "*Frijoles*, guacamole, fried bananas, tamales and flan for dessert. Come in, Papa is waiting for you in the backyard."

After sampling Antonio's special rum they sat down to dinner under the frangipani trees and ate the wonderful meal that Lupita had so painstakingly prepared. Music from the indoor stereo floated out into the yard, light flickered from lanterns and the bright slice of moon overhead.

"Have another tamale," Antonio said. "You don't eat enough. Maybe another piece of chicken?"

"Another bite and I'd fall into a stupor." Bree groaned. "This is the best meal I've had in fifteen years, Lupita. It was wonderful. Thank you for asking me."

"This is *tu casa*—your house," Antonio said. "You come back any time you want to. Next Saturday when everybody's here we'll roast a pig and fix paella." He filled Bree's cup with Cuban coffee. "Did you tell your mother she was invited, too?"

Bree nodded. "She said she'd come."

"That's good." With a chuckle he said, "I think it's time your mother and I signed a peace accord. Perhaps Saturday night will be the beginning of negotiations." He held his hand out to Bree. "You still know how to rumba?"

"Of course. Your wife was a good teacher." Bree reached across the table to touch his hand. "You must miss her."

"Every day of my life. She was a wonderful woman. Nothing has been the same without her." Antonio sighed, then with a shake of his head got to his feet and said, "Come on, let's see what you remember."

Antonio led her out to the patio and began to move with the music. "Aha," he said, "you *do* remember. Good, *muchacha*, very good." They danced for a minute or two before he said, "Come on, Miguel. Dance with Bree. Lupita, you dance with your papa."

It felt strange to have Miguel's arms around her. Bree smiled tentatively and breathlessly said, "It's been a long time."

Miguel nodded. It felt good to hold her this way. Her body felt light and strangely fragile against his. He caught the faint aroma of her perfume as they swayed together and she moved her hips enticingly to the Latin rhythm. He wanted to say something... anything. But he was unable to speak. Her hair brushed his cheek, soft and light and faintly scented. He tightened his hand around her waist and tried not to look at the rise of her breasts.

The music continued to drift on the soft night air. Bree caught the fragrance of gardenias and jasmine and, closing her eyes, leaned against Miguel's shoulder.

On a night like this Paris seemed a million miles away. The world narrowed down to this one place, this garden and this music and the feel of Miguel's hand against her back, the clasp of his other hand on hers.

He urged her closer. She sighed but didn't speak— she was lost in the music and the feel of his body against hers. When she finally raised her head and opened her eyes she saw that they were alone, but when she started to step away from him he tightened his arms around her.

The music stopped, but still he held her. She lifted her face and started to speak but he stopped her words with a kiss that warmed and shattered and weakened her knees. His lips were firm and demanding and hers softened and parted while a wonderful fire seeped into her bones. She felt his hands against her back, pressing her closer, and a trembling sigh escaped her lips. He took her sigh as his tongue moved into the warmth of her mouth. She heard the catch of his breath in his throat as he slid his hands up her arms and she swayed closer to him.

He let her go. "I didn't mean to do that," he murmured, as he stepped away from her.

Her arms felt empty without him. She looked up at Miguel, lost for a moment in the darkness of his eyes, wanting to touch the mouth that only a moment ago had covered hers with a strength and passion that had left her shaking with need. She didn't speak because she couldn't.

From the doorway Lupita called, "Dessert coming right up."

Bree turned away and with faltering steps found her way back to the table.

She ate the dessert, but she didn't taste it, or the cup of strong Cuban coffee that Antonio poured for her. She tried not to look at Miguel but couldn't help herself. His face looked tense and angry as he drummed his fingers restlessly against the tabletop.

At last he said, "I'm going out on the *Sweet Sue* at dawn, Dad. I'd better get going."

Antonio nodded and turned to Bree. "I hope you'll come back soon. Before the family get-together if you can."

"I'll try." She stood up to kiss his cheek, then to embrace Lupita. "Thank you. It was a wonderful dinner." She didn't look at Miguel.

He helped her into the car and drove without speaking. A block from her house he pulled over to the curb and turned the motor off.

Bree took a deep, shaking breath. "Why are you stopping?" she murmured. "What is it?"

"You know what it is," Miguel said as he reached for her. He put his hand against her hair, then with a muttered oath he pulled her into his arms.

His mouth crushed hers, hard and urgent, but with her whispered protest his lips softened against hers. When the kiss ended he put his hands on either side of her face and looked at her with eyes that were as black as the night that surrounded them. "You're so lovely," he murmured. His thumb brushed across her lips, and when, hesitatingly Bree touched the tip of her tongue to it, he whispered her name and slid his hands down to her shoulders. His expression softened and with a low groan he pulled her against him, kissing her again, more gently this time.

So gently that Bree became lost in the warmth of his mouth against hers and in the tender explorations of his tongue. She was so caught up in the stirring closeness she was almost unaware when he touched the soft roundness of her breasts. She wanted to pull away but his hands were warm against her skin as he caressed her.

"I've been mad with wanting to touch you like this, Bree," he whispered against her lips, and cupped her breasts through the thin fabric of her dress. He stopped whatever words of protest she would have uttered with a kiss that weakened her resistance.

He nipped the corners of her mouth and took her lower lip between his teeth to suckle and to lap, all the while warming her breasts in his hands and caressing the swollen peaks with his thumbs.

Bree brought her hands up to try to force him away. She'd flattened her hands against his chest, then, without thinking, unbuttoned his shirt to slip them inside and feel the warmth of his skin.

A shudder ran through Miguel when she touched him. He touched his tongue to her lips and when her lips parted and her tongue danced to meet his he groaned with pleasure.

A fierce, trembling heat swept through Bree's body as she moved closer to him. She was lost in the strength of the arms that held her, in the warmth of the mouth that possessed her. In the distance she heard the call of katydids and smelled the sweetness of night-blooming jasmine, and felt the beat of Miguel's heart under her hand. She moved her fingers to tangle in his chest hair and heard the breath rasp in his throat while she felt her own excitement build.

Suddenly—as suddenly as he'd taken her in his arms—Miguel let her go. He leaned his head back against the seat and spoke in a muffled voice. "I'm sorry. I shouldn't have done that. I..." The words faded and for a long moment he didn't speak. Finally, without a word, he started the car.

Bree looked straight ahead, as shaken as she'd ever been in her life. She didn't know what to say or do. She brushed the disheveled hair back from her face and tried to still her trembling lips. When Miguel stopped in front of her house she put one hand on the handle of the door. Without speaking he came around to help her out of the car and took her hand.

"I don't think we should let anything happen between us, Bree," he said without looking at her.

"What is it?" she whispered. "We used to be friends, Miguel. I'd like us to be...to be friends again."

"Friends?" Miguel looked at her. He took a long, shaking breath. Then he rested his hand against the side of her face. "Bree," he murmured. "Oh, Bree."

His body throbbed with the need to hold her again, but he knew he had to get away while there was still time—away from the questions he saw in her wide green eyes, away from her lips still swollen from his kisses.

"I'll call you," he said, forcing himself to turn away.

The scent of her lingered in the car. He rested his hand against the leather seat, felt her lingering warmth and tried to quell the terrible urgency that swelled in his body. What's happening to me? he asked himself as he turned the key in the ignition. He was no longer a lovesick boy and he had no intention of letting her hurt him again.

But that night, alone in his home by the beach, Miguel listened to the slow and steady roll of the sea. It seemed to him that every wave that crested whispered her name.

Chapter Four

Cornelia rose from the rocker when Bree opened the door. She glanced at the clock over the mantel and said, "It's late. I thought you'd be in—" She stopped and stared at Bree's unkempt hair before her gaze dropped to the dress that had slipped low over one shoulder. Her lips pursed in a disapproving frown. "So!"

The word resounded, humming like an off-key note in the silence of the room.

"I'm sorry I'm late. I didn't expect you to wait up for me."

"So?" That word again, this time a question. "Is it starting again? You and that Rivas boy?"

Bree smiled slightly. "Miguel isn't a boy, Mother, he's a man. And no, nothing is starting. Besides, it's certainly not *again* because there never was a *before*.

Miguel and I used to be friends and I'm fond of his family. That's all there is to it."

"That accounts for your dishevelment? Your coming in from a family dinner looking like...like that?" Cornelia thrust her chin forward. "You were *necking* with him!" she accused.

Bree's smile broadened. "Kids today use the term 'making out,' Mother." The smile faded and with a sigh she said, "Miguel kissed me good-night. You don't need to worry that it will go any further because I have a feeling he doesn't want it to—go further I mean." Bree brushed her hair back from her face and with a sigh said, "I'm tired, Mother. I don't want to talk about this now."

"But—"

Bree held up one hand. "Please," she said. "Not now." Then she climbed the stairs to her room and quietly closed the door.

She'd been telling her mother the truth when she'd said she was tired. She was, but it was more than tiredness that made her feel so enervated, so empty. It was as though every bit of strength had left her body when Miguel had turned and walked away from her tonight. He'd been angry when he'd kissed her and she didn't know why. Was it because there was someone else in his life, someone important to him, and he resented his father asking her to dinner? Then why had he kissed her at all?

Bree slipped out of her shoes and without undressing lay across the bed and stared up at the revolving fan that was a fixture in almost all Key West houses. Miguel's kiss had shaken her right down to her toes. She wasn't sure what would have happened if he hadn't let her go.

She closed her eyes and felt again the touch of his lips on hers. Why *had* he stopped? Hadn't he felt the same wonderful excitement, the need to be closer that she had felt? She'd touched his chest and sensed the rapid beating of his heart. She'd heard the excited rasp of his breath and felt his body tighten with need against hers. Then why? Why had he pushed her away from him? And what would she have done if he hadn't?

Finally Bree got up and undressed in the darkness of the room. But sleep didn't come because every time she closed her eyes she remembered the touch of Miguel's lips on hers. She touched her lips that still tingled from his kisses, and remembered the warmth of his hands on her. Finally, holding the thought of him close to her, Bree fell into a troubled sleep.

The Wednesday afternoon before the reunion Bree checked into the Beachcomber. She was given a room on the fifth floor with a balcony overlooking the pool and the Atlantic Ocean. She unpacked, changed to white pants and a yellow and white striped T-shirt and went down to the poolside restaurant to meet Dawn for lunch.

She hadn't heard from Miguel since she'd been to his father's house for dinner. She'd looked up his number in the telephone book and twice she'd picked up the phone to call him. But she hadn't gone through with it either time. Instead she sent flowers and a thank-you note to Antonio and Lupita.

As Bree made her way through the lobby and out to the patio, she wondered if she would see Miguel tomorrow night at the reception. She looked out at the umbrella-shaded tables for Dawn, and headed toward her. She paused when someone called her name, and with a smile hurried to the table where three women sat.

"Jean?" Bree laughed with pleasure as the woman stood up and hugged her. "Jean, you look wonderful," she said.

"So do you. You remember Frannie Buehler and Eleanor Mietz, don't you? Well, they used to be Buehler and Mietz. Frannie married Ed Lockhart and Ellie married a man from Gainsville. Her name's Ginsburg now and she has a darling little girl. You're still not married?"

Bree shook her head. "Nobody'll have me."

"Baloney," Jean said. "You live in Paris, don't you? That must be wonderful."

"It is, but it's nice to come home, too."

"You still think of this as home?" Frannie asked.

"Of course. I love Key West."

"Even during hurricane weather?" Eleanor made a face. "I guess you've heard one's brewing off the coast of Cuba."

"Really? The last I knew it was somewhere out in the Caribbean."

"According to this morning's newscast it's heading for Cuba," Eleanor said.

"Cuba's pretty close." Bree frowned.

"Ninety miles away," Jean said. "I hope the storm veers off. It'd be a shame to have to cancel the reunion."

"Maybe we should turn it into a long hurricane party." Frannie winked at Bree. "Candles and wine, a storm raging outside and all those dudes we haven't seen for fifteen years."

"Trees falling on the hotel and all of us in it, being blown out to sea!" Jean shuddered. "No, thanks."

Hugs were exchanged along with the promise to meet for breakfast the following morning. Then Bree made her way to Dawn's table.

"Old home week," she said as she sat down. "I just ran into Jean Schwan, Frannie Buehler and Eleanor Mietz. They said the hurricane was getting closer. What'll we do if it hits?"

"Run for higher ground," Dawn said. "But it won't hit, Bree. You know yourself that this time of year there's always a hurricane threatening to hit the Florida coast. But it usually veers out to sea or zigzags on up to the Carolinas." She made a face. "I don't even want to think about it, but I'll check with the weather service right after breakfast." She looked around at the other tables, saw someone she knew and waved. "It's fun, isn't it? Seeing all these people you haven't seen in years?"

"More fun than I thought it would be. After the other night with Gwen I was ready to take the first plane back to Paris."

"She's not always like that, but sometimes once she starts you just can't turn her off. I shouldn't have invited her but she's on the food committee and I had to. I've been meaning to tell you how sorry I am about the way she behaved."

Bree shrugged. "It doesn't matter. She ignored me all through high school; I've decided to ignore her now."

"Good for you. How was dinner at the Rivas house?"

"Wonderful." Bree took a sip from the cup of coffee a waiter had placed beside her plate. "It was good to see Lupita again. She's quite lovely and Antonio's a terrific host."

"And?"

"And what?"

Dawn leaned forward. "I'm waiting to hear about Miguel."

"What about Miguel?"

"Oh, come on, Bree! I saw the way he looked at you the night you came for dinner and in the office at the dock." Dawn giggled. "His eyes were absolutely smoldering with passion."

"Oh, come on!" Bree shook her head in exasperation, but she couldn't stop the color that flushed her face.

"So what happened?" Dawn asked. "Did he drive you home? Have you been out with him since?"

Bree set the cup on the saucer and picked up a menu. "Yes, he took me home. And no, I haven't seen him since the dinner at his father's."

"Why not?"

"Because he hasn't called, he hasn't asked me out."

"I'll be damned." Dawn looked surprised.

Bree hesitated, wondering how to phrase the question she wanted to ask. Finally she just came out with it. "Is there anyone special in Miguel's life? I mean . . . is he involved in a relationship?"

Dawn shook her head as she reached for a cinnamon roll. "He's been involved off and on, but there's nobody special that I know of now. I get the idea that the minute a woman gets serious he backs off." She looked up as the waiter approached, glanced at the menu and said, "Fresh strawberries, French toast and crisp bacon. What about you, Bree?"

"That sounds good." Bree smiled up at the waiter. "I'll have the same."

When the waiter disappeared Dawn said, "Miguel's always been a loner, Bree. I remember when he and his parents first came here from Cuba that he didn't have much to do with the other kids. It must have been hard on him, and on the other Cuban kids, too—being refugees, I mean, not speaking very good English. You tutored Miguel for a while, didn't you?"

"For about a year. We got to be good friends. At least I thought we were friends. He went into the navy before I left the Keys to go to school and he didn't even tell me goodbye. And now..." She let the words hang in the air.

"And now what?"

"I don't know, Dawn. I have a feeling he's backing away. It's almost as though he doesn't like me."

"That's silly, Bree. Of course Miguel likes you. I wasn't kidding when I said his eyes were smoldering the other day at his office. He couldn't keep them off you." Dawn shrugged. "Maybe he's just busy."

"Maybe." But Bree knew that wasn't the reason. Whatever it was, she decided, she was going to find out. She would see Miguel tomorrow night at the reception and she intended to discover his reasons for keeping his distance.

Bree had bought her dress for the reception last month in Paris. It was a white silk chemise, cut low in the back, held up by thin straps of beaded gold. Her only jewelry was a gold chain and button earrings. She brushed her hair back off her face and held it in place with two golden combs before she stepped into her white pumps and looked at herself in the mirror.

"Okay," she said to her reflection. "You're not in high school any more. You're not too tall, you're not too thin—and your heels are *not* too high.'' She frowned at the mirror and wondered why she was so suddenly overwhelmed with doubts about herself.

She'd been fine these past few years in Paris, secure and accepting of herself the way she was. Now suddenly all of her uncertainties were back. It was as though she was seventeen again, just as awkward and insecure as she'd been when she was young. Was that what coming home meant?

With a sigh Bree snapped the light off and the room was filled with moonlight and the reflection of patio lights as she opened the door to the balcony and stepped outside. The night was soft and scents from the garden below perfumed the air. She took a deep breath as she rested her hands on the railing and gazed down at the sparkling water of the pool, the swaying palms, and beyond to the sea.

While there was a joy in returning home, there was also a feeling of melancholy for the years that had passed and for the friends who had changed—as she had changed. Many of them, like Dawn and John, had been married for over ten years. Others had children. She didn't envy them but she knew that her time was running out for a family.

Bree tightened her hands on the balcony railing. You can't have everything, she told herself. She had an exciting career and lived in one of the most beautiful cities in the world. That surely made up for what she'd missed, didn't it? Slowly Bree shook her head. Did anything make up for all the lonely nights she'd spent in the past fifteen years? For the children she didn't have?

She wondered why tonight of all nights she had a touch of the blues. Then, impatient with herself, she left the balcony and went back into the room just as there was a knock at the door. She opened it and a hotel employee handed her a small, square florist's box. "Miss Brianna Petersen?" he asked.

Through the cellophane Bree could see a cluster of pink camellias. When the messenger left she opened the box and looked for a card. There wasn't one, but she didn't need one to know who had sent them.

Bree went to the mirror and removed the gold combs from her hair, brushed it loose again and fastened the camellias behind one ear.

Once again she looked at her reflection, with a smile now because Miguel had remembered that night so long ago.

Only the members of the committee had arrived when Bree entered the Banyan Room where the reception was to be held. Dawn and Jean Schwan were checking out the buffet table, and Gwen was giving orders to the musicians. A man Bree didn't know stood talking to the bartender.

"It's almost time," Dawn said when she saw Bree. "You look gorgeous. Is the dress from Paris?"

Bree nodded. "Is it all right?"

"No, it'd look better on me." Dawn grinned and led her over to a long table covered with name tags. "This is your post," she told Bree. "Carris Nelson will be here with you. You'll probably recognize everybody, but if you don't, don't be afraid to ask their names. We've all changed in fifteen years." She looked up as a slender man of medium height entered the room. "Hi, Carris," she called. "Over here." "You remember Bree Petersen, don't you?"

"Sure. Hi, Bree. Great to see you again." Carris looked toward the door and said, "Oh, Lord, here they come. Brace yourself, Bree."

The next twenty minutes zipped by in a blur of half-remembered names and faces. There were shrieked greetings, hugs and appraisals. To her surprise, and in spite of the fact that fifteen years had gone by, Bree recognized almost everybody. She and Carris handed out name tags and greetings, and every time another man appeared at the table, Bree looked up, expecting to see Miguel.

But she wasn't prepared when suddenly Craig Logan stood before her. "Bree?" he said. "My God, Bree, is it really you?"

She turned from the person she'd been speaking to. Craig clasped her hand, his eyes wide with surprise. Slowly he shook his head. "I'll be damned," he said. "You've turned into a knockout. When did you get here? How long are you staying?"

"I've been here for a week." Bree withdrew her hand and turned to the table to find his name tag. "I'll be here another week or so."

"Great. Let's have dinner tonight as soon as this shindig is over."

"I don't think so, Craig. There'll be a lot of straightening up to do after the reception."

"That's okay, I'll hang around."

Bree looked at him and for the briefest fraction of a second her eyes showed the surprise she felt. Craig had changed, and not for the better. He was still handsome, but in a harried, worn sort of way. There were dark patches under his eyes and lines around his mouth. His jacket, obviously expensive, stretched too tightly across his shoulders and there was just the faintest suggestion of a fullness of stomach that, without care, would soon develop into a potbelly.

"We can eat here at the hotel if you'd like. They serve until ten," he said after lighting a cigarette. He glanced toward the door and his dark brows drew together in a frown. "Oh, damn it," he muttered angrily. "I'll catch you later."

Bree looked toward the door as Craig moved away. Standing there alone, almost as though she was afraid to enter, was Bobbie Lee Dillon Logan. She looked at the crowd, saw Craig turning toward the bar and hesitated. Then, as though steeling herself, she moved toward the reception table.

"Hey, Bobbie Lee," Carris said. "How're you doing? Great to see you."

"You too, Carris." Bobbie cleared her throat. "Hi, Bree. Remember me?"

"Of course, Bobbie. How are you?"

"Fine." She stood awkwardly by the table, fiddling nervously with the buttons on her size sixteen dress. Cute little Bobbie Lee Dillon—the almost ex-Mrs. Craig Logan—had spread to a fullness of figure that both shocked and dismayed Bree.

Bobbie Lee pinned the name tag on her dress with trembling fingers. She stood there a moment uncertainly and said, "Well, I...I guess I'll have a drink. It's nice seeing you again, Bree."

"You too, Bobbie." Bree hesitated. "Look," she said, "I'll be finished here in a few minutes. I'll join you at the bar."

"Okay." Bobbie's face lightened in a smile. She crossed her arms over her chest. "I'll see you then."

"If there's one thing that gal doesn't need it's another drink." Carris shook his head. "I don't suppose the divorce is doing her any good." He looked around the room, then at the few remaining name tags on the table. "Another five minutes should do it," he told Bree. "If anybody else comes in they can find their own tags. I want to get over to that buffet table before everything's cleaned out."

"You go ahead," Bree said. "I'll stay here a little while longer."

"Are you sure?"

Bree nodded. "Yes, go on." When Carris left she looked around her at the women and men she'd grown up with and at their husbands and wives. With a smothered sigh Bree arranged the few remaining name tags. Just as she picked up her evening bag and started around the table, Miguel appeared.

"Sorry I'm late," he said as he stopped in front of the table. "There was a problem with one of the boats." He picked up his tag and pinned it to his white jacket. "I hate these damn things," he said.

"So do I. That's why I put it on my bag."

Miguel nodded. "I can see why you wouldn't want to put it on your dress." He hesitated. "You look beautiful tonight, Bree."

She wanted to compliment him, as well, and wondered why she had an overwhelming desire to rest her hand against the side of his face. Instead she thanked him for the camellias.

"You're welcome."

"You remembered."

"Of course I remembered."

Miguel looked at her and suddenly he wanted to take her hand and lead her to some quiet place where he could put his arms around her and touch her through the softness of her dress. He wanted to feel the sweet curves and planes of her body, to loosen her hair and curl it around his fingers as he drew her close.

Because he couldn't touch her he touched the camellias. Tucking a tendril of hair behind her ear, he said, "I suppose we'd better join the party."

"Yes." Bree took a deep breath. She looked up at him, then away. Searching for something to say she said, "What's the latest news of the storm?"

"It's an official hurricane now, dubbed Lola by the weathermen. The last I heard she'd veered away from Cuba and was headed toward the Bahamas."

"Then it won't hit the Keys."

"It's too early to tell yet, Bree. Hurricanes are funny. Lola could suddenly turn around and head straight for us or just as suddenly run out of steam." He glanced down at the two names left on the table. "You about through here?"

"Yes. I told Bobbie I'd meet her at the bar."

Miguel nodded. "I'll walk you over." He took her arm, hesitated, then said, "What are you doing for dinner?"

"Craig asked me to have dinner with him. I—"

"Fine." Miguel's face tightened and he didn't speak as they made their way to the bar. Then, in a coldly polite voice he asked Bree what she would like to drink.

"A glass of white wine, please," she said.

He ordered two glasses, handed one to Bree and started to edge away. But someone jostled his arm and when he turned he was face to face with Craig Logan.

"Oops, sorry. Oh, it's you. Hi, Mike, how're ya doing?" Craig put his arm around Bree's waist. "What do you think about Bree? Isn't she a knockout?'' He gave her a squeeze. "How'd I ever let you get away from me, gorgeous?"

She tried to move away, but his arm tightened. "Couldn't see the beauty for the beasts," he said. He glanced toward Bobbie Lee, who stood alone at the other end of the bar, holding a drink with both hands.

Bree pulled away from him. "Excuse me," she said to Miguel, then quickly moved toward Bobbie. Forcing a cheerful tone she said, "Some party, isn't it?"

Bobbie nodded. She downed her drink and ordered another one. Her eyes darted to Craig, then away. "I shouldn't have come," she murmured. "It's too awkward. Craig and I...'' She stared down at her drink and her chin trembled.

"I know that you've separated," Bree said. "I'm sorry."

"I guess it's better this way. He's been so unhappy these last few years, and I...I'm to blame. I should have tried harder. I should have..." She drank half of her drink in one long gulp. She looked at Bree. "You look so pretty," she said.

"Thanks, Bobbie." Bree laced her arm through the other woman's. "Let's go try the buffet table, shall we? I've got a taste for shrimp." Before Bobbie could object, Bree led her away from the bar. And although she talked to other friends during the evening, she stayed close to Bobbie's side.

She was dismayed at the way the other woman looked. Bobbie Lee had been one of the cutest girls in her class. Cute. Damn, there was that word again! But in Bobbie's case it was true. She'd worn her chestnut hair short and curly, her figure had been great, she'd been as friendly as a puppy and—like Bree—she'd adored Craig Logan.

What happens to people? Bree wondered. What happens to make love turn into that kind of unhappiness, that kind of despair?

It was toward the end of the evening when Miguel asked her to dance.

"You've been mother-henning Bobbie," he said. "That's nice of you."

"She's changed so much, Miguel."

"We've all changed." He tightened his arms around her.

"When will their divorce be final?"

He looked at her and the anger came back to his dark eyes. "Why? Are you going to stick around and see you if can snag Craig the second time around?"

"No! No, of course not!" Bree stepped away from him, as angry as he was now and determined to find out why he was behaving the way he was.

But before she could ask, Miguel said, "Sorry, that was uncalled for. I suddenly remembered you had a crush on Craig. I guess that made me mad."

"Fifteen years ago!" Bree said indignantly.

"Okay." Miguel put his hand on the back of her head, bringing her cheek against his shoulder. Forcing the anger out of his voice he said, "Remember this song?"

She listened to the remembered strains of "The First Time Ever I Saw Your Face" and nodded. "We danced to this at the prom, didn't we?"

Miguel took a deep breath. She was so lovely that night. He'd held her in his arms, and wanted desperately to tell her how much he loved her. But she'd only had eyes for Craig.

He looked over her shoulder now and saw Craig watching them. Just as Craig started toward them

Miguel said, "How'd you like to go sailing tomorrow?"

Bree looked up at him, pleased. "I'd love to," she said. "But what about the beach party?"

"Stay for an hour, then meet me down at the dock. One o'clock?"

"Yes, fine. I'll—"

Craig tapped Miguel's shoulder. "My turn," he said.

Miguel stepped away from Bree, but for a moment he tightened his hand on hers. "Tomorrow," he said.

Chapter Five

It seemed to Bree that there had never been a day so full of promise. She stood on her balcony looking out over the pool and the beach where the class of '72 had already begun to gather for the beach party. The sky was a clear, clean blue, accented with soft, white clouds. Sailboats skimmed the waves, their sails billowing in the gentle off-shore breeze.

In a little while Bree would go down and join her former classmates and friends, but for now she was content to rest here on the balcony, sipping her morning coffee while she watched the activity below. Dressed in white sharkskin shorts and a jade green T-shirt that matched her eyes, she was ready for both the beach party and the sailing date with Miguel. She'd stay at the beach for an hour, then come back to her room to pick up the canvas bag containing her swimsuit, her camera and a straw sun hat.

She wasn't sure why Miguel had invited her to go sailing—whether he'd asked her to go with him because he really wanted to be with her, or whether he felt an obligation to entertain an out-of-town friend.

Bree stood up and leaned against the railing. She thought of how it would be when she was alone with Miguel, and in spite of the warmth of the sun on her skin, she shivered with anticipation.

Miguel wasn't like the men she was used to, suave Frenchmen with polished manners and a charming way with words. There wasn't anything suave about Miguel. He was straightforward and almost frighteningly masculine. He'd kissed her with a passion that had left her shaking with need and frightened, more of herself than of him. What would it be like, she wondered, to spend a whole day alone with him, far from shore, far from their friends?

When Bree went down to the beach party she tried not to look at her watch. But she did, again and again, until finally Dawn asked, "What's the matter? You're acting like you're in a hurry to go some place."

"I am," Bree confessed. "I'm going sailing with Miguel."

"Aha!"

"What's that supposed to mean?"

Dawn grinned. "Nothing, dear, just aha."

"Sure." Bree glanced at her watch again. "I guess I'd better get going," she said.

Dawn didn't attempt to hide her smile. "Have a good time. Give me a buzz when you get back."

"I will." Bree hesitated. She saw Craig, who'd just arrived, heading her way and said to Dawn, "I'd rather you didn't tell anybody where I'm going, okay?"

"I won't say a word. You'd better get going before Craig nabs you. Say hi to Miguel for me."

Bree nodded. She waved to Craig with a brief greeting and hurried into the hotel before he could stop her.

It took her only a few minutes to drive to the marina. When she parked she walked out onto the pier where dozens of boats were moored. She looked around, then saw Miguel. He was wearing white denim pants and was bare-chested. Because he was working on the boat he didn't see her and for a moment Bree studied him unobserved. His tall body was trim and spare, without an ounce of extra fat. She could see the muscles in his arms and across his back as he worked—not the bulging muscles of a weight lifter, but the finely honed muscles of a man in peak condition.

When Miguel spotted her he jumped from his yawl moored near the end of the pier and hurried toward her.

"I didn't know the name of your boat," Bree said. "I wasn't sure what to look for."

"And I wasn't sure you'd get away from the party so soon." He took the canvas bag. "Come on. The wind's up and it's a great day for a sail. Have you had lunch yet?"

"No, I wasn't hungry."

"Good. Lupita packed something for us, we'll eat later." He led Bree down the pier to the forty-foot boat.

"She's beautiful." Bree stopped and gazed at the boat. She read the name, *Straight On Till Morning*, emblazoned in gold and black letters. "That's nice, Miguel. It sounds familiar but I'm not sure why."

"It's from *Peter Pan*. Wendy asks Peter how to get to Never Never Land and Peter says, 'Second star on the right, straight on till morning.'" He put his hands in the pockets of his white pants. "I read a lot of children's books when we first came to Florida because they were easier to understand. That line stayed in my mind—because it was a childhood fantasy, I guess. It meant something special to me about keeping on until you've reached your goal and not giving up until you've found your dream."

"And did you?" Bree asked. "Did you find your dream, Miguel?"

"Not yet." He looked at her and for a moment his face was unguarded and vulnerable. Then he turned away and jumped lightly into the boat.

When he helped her aboard Bree said, "Where are we headed?"

"I thought we'd sail toward the Dry Tortugas. Okay with you?"

"Yes, I haven't been there since I was a kid. When Dad belonged to the yacht club a whole group of people sailed there one weekend. I was about eleven, I think. I remember we went to Garden Key to see Fort Jefferson and that I had nightmares for weeks about how grim the prison was and how unfair I thought it was to have imprisoned poor Dr. Mudd there."

Miguel smiled because he remembered how Bree had looked when he'd first seen her, shortly after he and his family had come from Cuba. At eleven she'd been a solemn child with flaxen hair and a shy, bewitching smile. He could just imagine her, listening to the story of the physician who'd been sent to this remote island prison because he'd set the broken leg of the man who shot Lincoln. Her head would have been cocked to one side; her green eyes would have been serious and troubled.

Miguel was still smiling as he maneuvered the boat out of the slip and headed toward the open sea. It was a beautiful day, a day to relish being alive in, and he was with Bree. At least for today she was his.

There was a slight chop to the water. The wind was brisk and the sun turned Bree's pale skin a wonderful rosy color. Her hair blew back from her face and he found himself wanting to lace his fingers through the silky blond strands. And yes, God help him, he wanted to kiss the lips parted now in pleasure and run his hands underneath the T-shirt that fit snugly against her breasts. He took a deep, calming breath. ''You'd better put on sun block.''

She moved to find her bag, then returned to sit near him by the tiller. ''I know I look like a real snowbird,'' she said as she rubbed sunscreen on her face. ''I've been meaning to get to the beach but Dawn's kept me too busy working on the reunion.''

''I guess you enjoyed seeing your old friends.'' Miguel hesitated. ''Where'd you and Craig have dinner last night?''

''We didn't. I went up to Dawn and John's room after the party and we sent down for hamburgers.''

''But you said you were going to dinner with him.''

''I said he asked me—I didn't say I was going.'' Bree averted her face. ''If you'd waited around a little longer you'd have known that.''

But he hadn't waited around. He'd left the party long before she had and he'd taken Bobbie Lee home. Bree had been grateful for that. Even though she'd tried to keep an eye on Craig's wife, Bobbie had managed to drink more than she should have. Bree, unable to get away, had looked for Craig. But it was Miguel who stepped in to help. "I'll see that she gets home safely," he'd told Bree and with gentle persuasion had taken Bobbie's arm and said, "Come on, pal, let me take you home."

The thought of her high-school girlfriend saddened Bree. What turns a lovely, happy young girl into an alcoholic? she wondered. Why had Bobbie let herself go? Was it because of the divorce or was the divorce because of the way she looked? Bree felt sorry for both Bobbie and Craig, but today was supposed to be an escape and she tried to put the thought of the unhappy couple out of her mind.

When the wind began to lessen, Miguel headed for a small island and said, "How about a swim?"

"Wonderful." Bree looked around her as Miguel lowered the anchor. "This is a beautiful spot."

"You can go below and change. I've already got my trunks on." Miguel began to lower the sails and by the time Bree returned he'd pulled off his pants and was standing by the rail waiting for her.

He looked at her and the breath caught in his throat. The strapless bathing suit, in variegated colors of blue and turquoise and green, fit her slender body like a second skin. Her breasts were small and high. Her legs were as perfect as he remembered and there was a flare to her hips that excited him. She'd pinned her hair up, and standing there, poised and waiting, she looked like a pale and lovely princess.

"You look . . ." Miguel took a deep breath. "You look like a Viking princess," he said. "Ready?" His voice sounded almost harsh in the quiet of the day.

He waited until Bree nodded, then he stepped over the rail and dove into the water. "It's great," he said

when he surfaced and shook the water from his face.
"Come on."

He looked up at her as she stepped to the edge of the
boat and his body warmed and tightened with need.
She raised her arms above her head, arched her body
and cut through the water next to him. She came up
sputtering with laughter. "You're right—it is wonderful." She grinned at him. "I'll race you to the
island."

Bree was a good swimmer. Her arms reached out,
cutting cleanly, swiftly through the water, and it took
every bit of his strength to pull ahead of her. When at
least he felt the sand under his feet he said, "You swim
a hell of a race, lady."

"But you beat me," she said, gasping for breath.

"By about two inches.

"I'm out of shape." She rested a hand on his
shoulder.

"Your shape looks pretty good to me."

Bree took her hand off his shoulder and when he
asked if she wanted to explore the island she shook her
head. "No, let's swim."

They swam leisurely, side by side, until at last Miguel said, "I'm hungry. How about you?"

"Starving." She stroked easily beside him, then
quickly away as she headed back to the boat.

Miguel held back so that he could watch her. When
she reached the boat she clung to the side of it. Drop-
lets of water sparkled against her skin. Her eyes,
framed by long dark lashes pearled with drops of water, were as green as the sea.

Miguel took a deep breath, then unable to help
himself he put his arms around her. Her skin was sleek
and wet against his as she lifted her face for his kiss.

Bree closed her eyes, then opened them to look at Miguel before she released her grip on the side of the boat and let her body float alongside his. With one hand against the small of her back, he pressed her so close he could feel every line of her body. When she gasped he kissed her, relishing the taste of her lips and the touch of her body.

Bree closed her eyes as she clung to him, almost unaware as they sank beneath the turquoise water, lost in the magic of his kiss and the feel of his hard masculine body so close to hers.

They rose to the surface, gasping for air, but before Bree could speak Miguel kissed her again, and when her mouth opened under his he slipped his tongue past her salt-slick lips into the moistness of her mouth.

A wave threatened to part them and when it did, Miguel pressed her closer again. His body was in a rage of desire and he throbbed with wanting her. He knew that she could feel his arousal through the thinness of the fabric that separated them and he murmured her name against her lips as he pulled down the top of her swim suit.

Her breasts were cool against his chest, the hardened nipples pressed cold against his skin. He wound his legs around hers and he was lost in her, drowning in her. Her arms urged him closer. She caressed his shoulders and the fine hairs at the back of his neck and he murmured with pleasure.

Bree felt the heat of her body simmering in the coolness of the water. When Miguel pressed her closer still she felt the strength of his masculinity against her and clung to him—her breasts against his chest, her mouth tight to his. Together they sank once more beneath the surface of the water into the silence of the sea, two earth creatures wrapped in each other's arms, strangely at home here in this quiet and alien place.

When I die, Miguel thought, I want it to be like this. But no, he didn't want to die with her, he wanted to live with her. To live out all the days of his life with his beloved Bree.

They rose to the surface and with his arms still around her he said, "Let's go aboard."

"Yes." Her voice trembled and she put her hand on his shoulder.

He climbed aboard first, then helped her up. For a moment they only looked at each other. Then he reached around and took the pins from her hair.

The sun burned down but Bree felt herself shiver. She knew what would happen now, knew that she wanted it more than anything in the world and felt weak with longing. Her body ached with a hunger she'd never before experienced. In a moment Miguel would lead her below and strip her suit away.

Bree paused in surprise when instead he led her to a stack of towels. He spread them on the teak deck and turned to her. Slowly, he pulled the wet suit down over her body, then held her away from him so that he could look at her.

"Miguel..." She felt as though she'd never breathe properly again. "Someone will see."

"We're alone, Bree." He drew her into his arms and gently eased her down to the deck. He kissed her sweet mouth again, he tasted her with slow, deepening sips, and felt her hunger grow.

Her body was sea damp against his and when the kisses weren't enough, when he knew he had to touch her naked body with his own, he rolled away from her and stripped out of his swim trunks. He knelt beside her, gazing down at the pale perfection of her body. This was his Bree, naked and trembling before him. This was what he'd always dreamed of.

Miguel kissed her again and when she lifted her arms to encircle his neck his heart swelled with gladness because she wanted this as much as he did. In a moment their bodies would be joined and all of his boyhood fantasies would be fulfilled. But for a moment yet he would hold back—there was a heightened pleasure in the waiting now that he was sure of what was to come.

He cupped her cool breasts, holding them poised and ready for his hungry mouth as he trailed kisses around her ears and down her throat. Her body quivered beneath his.

Her breasts tasted of salt. He lapped at them, licking the tender roundness before he took one peaked blossom between his lips. He heard the soft moan tumble from her mouth, and swelled with the knowledge that at last, after all these years, he could touch her like this. His body was on fire with a passion he hadn't thought possible. His teeth tightened on one rosy tip and his tongue flickered hard against it. Bree cried out and his body tightened with pleasure.

Pleasure. She'd never dreamed...she hadn't known that anything could be like this. She raised her body to Miguel's, offering him the feast of her small round breasts. She threaded her fingers through the blackness of his hair, not even aware of the sounds coming from her mouth—her small, frantic cries of delight, her whispered pleas for more.

Miguel rolled her onto her side so that while he kissed her he could stroke the flare of her hips and her thighs. He found her silken warmth with his fingers, then gasped with pleasure when she tentatively caressed his hips and belly in gentle strokes. He thought he would die with the joy of it.

This was the dream, this the fulfillment. He whispered her name and touched her face the way a blind man would, remembering, memorizing her beauty.

The boat moved gently on the waves. The sun shone down on their naked bodies while water splashed against the hull. Bree was lost somewhere between sky and sea, merging with the universe as she clung to Miguel. She lifted her body to his, almost beside herself with the wonder of the feeling he was giving her, with this incredible passion that made them cling so breathlessly to each other.

He reached for her mouth and she knew she'd never been kissed like this before. She whispered his name and felt his breath rasp with pleasure.

His strokes deepened, quickened. His hands tightened on her body. She gasped and pleaded—not even sure what she pleaded for until suddenly the sky and the sea merged to crush her between them and her body lifted, spiraling higher and higher. She wasn't aware that she'd cried his name or that he'd exclaimed, "*Ay Dios*, Bree, how I love you!" just before his body exploded into hers.

She clung to him, afraid that if she didn't she wouldn't be able to hang on to reality. His body tightened against hers as together they weathered the passion that shook them, one with the sun and the sea and with the gulls that glided against the azure sky.

Afterward they lay side by side, drifting with the gentle motion of the boat. No words were necessary. Miguel took a hand and brought it to his lips. He kissed each finger, as content as he had ever been in his life because Bree was beside him and because for now, for this one day, she was his.

He'd known other women in his thirty-four years, but never before had he experienced such a sweetness of passion. Never before had a woman clung to him or whispered his name as Bree had whispered it. Suddenly he was shaken by a deep sadness. Bree wasn't his and soon she'd leave him. She'd go back to Paris and to the life she had there and he would remain here in Key West, without her.

They lay quietly while she drowsed against him, only half aware of the sun on her naked body and of his hand, strong and firm on her flesh, as he gently caressed her. Just before she turned the corner into sleep he said, "You'd better move into the shade."

Bree summoned a halfhearted "Um."

Miguel sat up. "Come on, Bree. You're getting pink. How'll you explain a sunburned bottom to your mother?"

She opened her eyes and a blush that wasn't from the sun flooded her cheeks. "I guess you're right," she said, and reached for her bathing suit.

Miguel pulled his trunks on. "Hungry?" he asked as he moved into the shade.

"Famished."

"Then let's go below and eat. While I'm setting the table you can shower."

When Bree came out of the shower, her clean hair was wrapped in a towel. She'd put her shorts and the T-shirt back on, and she was barefoot. The table, set with unbreakable dishes, was filled with several kinds of cheese, cold fried chicken, roast beef, pickles and Cuban bread.

"Wine or beer?" Miguel asked.

"Beer, I think." Bree slid into the seat. "This looks wonderful."

They ate quietly, just enjoying the feel of the sea beneath them and their newfound intimacy. When they finished Bree said, "I'll clean up if you tell me where things go."

Miguel nodded. "The cupboards are here," he told her. "Soap and dishpan under there." He glanced at the clock over the sink. "We'd better be on our way," he said as he started up the stairs. Then he turned back and coming to Bree he put a finger under her chin and raising her face for a kiss said, "It was wonderful, Bree. More, so much more than anything I've ever experienced."

He went up on deck, pulled the anchor up, then raised the sails. The wind, sharper than it had been an hour ago, billowed them out, full and white. Miguel braced his feet with his hand on the tiller. The wind felt good on his face, and it cleared his head. Well, almost. He felt bemused, foolishly happy. Every part of his body was alive, zinging with joy and a sense of fulfillment that he'd never felt before.

Bree had bewitched him and taken him to a place he'd never been before. A happy grin spread over Miguel's face. She was his dream come true, his Wendy—she'd taken him to Never Never Land and he wouldn't be the same again.

When she came up she sat in the sun, her still-damp hair blowing in the wind so that it would dry. Her face and arms were pink and he let her hold the tiller while he spread sunscreen on her. "You'd better do your own legs," he said. "If I do them we'll never get to the Tortugas."

Bree smiled at him and something, he wasn't sure what, clutched at his heart. He kissed her again, then standing behind her, his arms encircling her, took the tiller. She smelled of fresh air and sunlight, and an elusive scent that was particularly her own. He rested his face against her hair. "I like the way you smell," he said. "I like the way you feel in my arms."

Bree leaned back against him and closed her eyes. Nothing will ever be as good as this, she thought. She'd always remember this day, the feel of the sun on her face, and the warmth of Miguel's arms around her.

A freighter passed in the distance, the smoke from its stacks spiraling into the clear blue sky. A school of flying fish leapt alongside the boat, and a slow brown shark moved sluggishly beside them.

The wind picked up, the chop of the waves grew stronger and splashed up over the bow. Almost without warning the sky darkened.

"Hold her steady for a minute," Miguel said. "I'm going below to check the weather."

He almost ran to the stairs leading to the cabin. Damn! The weather had turned bad and he hadn't even noticed. He'd put the squelch button on the radio when he and Bree had gone swimming but he'd meant to turn it back up as soon as they were in the boat. Then he'd kissed Bree and all hell had broken loose.

Miguel switched on the marine radio. "This is *Straight On Till Morning*, out of Key West, heading to the Tortugas," he said. "I've just sighted the Pulaski Shoal Marker, aiming toward East Key and the entrance to Southeast Channel. I'm picking up thirty-knot winds and four- to five-foot waves. Can you advise weather conditions please?''

"Stand by," a static-laden voice said. "We have small-craft warnings out because of a tropical storm. Suggest you call ranger station at Fort Jefferson for information."

"Thank you. *Straight On Till Morning* out." Miguel's forehead furrowed with worry as he fiddled with the dial. In another minute he heard the voice from the ranger station at Fort Jefferson confirm his call. "I read you. What is your position?"

"I've just sighted the Pulaski Shoal Marker. What's the latest weather info?"

"We've got a tropical storm formation. Strong winds and high seas. Situation should diminish by morning. Suggest you proceed to north side of Fort Jefferson to ride out the storm."

"Roger, will do. Thanks. Over and out."

Miguel flicked the off switch and glared at the radio. How could he have been so irresponsible? He'd checked weather conditions before they left Key West but there was a hurricane brewing somewhere out in the Caribbean and any sailor worth his salt would have checked again. He'd left the radio turned to channel sixteen, of course, but then he'd been too wrapped up to pay attention to the weather.

Now, because he hadn't, he'd exposed Bree to danger. He'd have to tell her they wouldn't be able to make it to Key West tonight, that they'd have to spend the night moored off Fort Jefferson.

The night.

But in spite of the prospect of spending the night on the boat with Bree, Miguel cursed under his breath.

He'd find a cove or an inlet where they'd be safe until the storm passed. They'd spend the night there, snug and safe in each other's arms.

Miguel closed his eyes at the thought.

Then he hurried up the stairs to the deck.

Chapter Six

By the time they neared Fort Jefferson the wind had risen to a howling gale. Rain lashed them and waves roared over the hull. Miguel told Bree to go below but she refused. She loved the thrilling force of the sea beneath them and grabbed up her camera—capturing the fierce blend of water and sky. Her expression was unafraid, her eyes bright with excitement.

"No motion sickness?"

Bree shook her head, and with a laugh said, "Vikings never get seasick."

She wasn't afraid because she was with Miguel. He would get them to a safe harbor.

But she was concerned about her mother. She looked at Miguel and put down the camera. Over the force of the wind she said, "My mother's going to be frantic. I told her we were going sailing today and that I'd phone her as soon as we returned."

"I'll have the marine radio call my dad the minute we find a place that's safe from the storm, Bree. He'll get in touch with your mother." Miguel pushed his wet, windblown hair back out of his eyes. "This is my fault; I should have checked the weather earlier."

A foam-crested wave slashed up over the bow. Bree tightened her hand around a strut. "No, it's my fault," she said. "You were too otherwise occupied to think about the weather."

A flame shot through Miguel's body. He looked at her rain-wet face, at the glorious mane of hair flying in the wind, and his hands tightened on the tiller. She was a woman he'd thought too cool, too shy and vulnerable, too remote for love and lovemaking. He'd been wrong, Bree wasn't like that at all. There she stood, her fine body leaning into the wind, her face alive with excitement. The memory of what had passed between them today shook him. He took one hand off the tiller and almost roughly put a hand behind her neck and pulled her to him. "Sea witch," he murmured, before his mouth crushed hers in a kiss that was as wild as the sea that surrounded them.

Soon, God willing, they would find a safe harbor, and when they did, when the boat was secure and they were safe, he would make love to her again. He would do to her all of the things he'd ever wanted to do to a woman. For now, for today and tonight, she belonged to him.

The sky darkened. Miguel gave the tiller to Bree while he reefed the sails and threw out the sea anchor that would act as a drag to slow their movements. Through the slash of rain he could barely make out the buoy markers. Bree helped to spot them and called their locations.

Finally through the wind and the rain he saw Fort Jefferson. He brought the boat in as close to the island as he dared, then maneuvered toward the leeward side until he found a sheltered place near the bank. Then he quickly lowered the sails and dropped double anchors. There would be a drag, but with luck they wouldn't drift too far. When he was sure the boat was secure, he brought Bree below deck.

Miguel handed her one of his cotton shirts and sent her to dry off. "This ought to do it," he said as he headed for the shower. "Why don't you fix us some supper? The coffee's on and there's canned food in the cupboards over the stove."

Bree nodded and when he disappeared she quickly slipped on the shirt. She towel dried her hair, then brushed it back off her face in a ponytail.

There were still two pieces of chicken and a little cheese left from the lunch Lupita had packed. Bree searched through the cupboard, found a can of baked beans but discovered she had no idea how to light the stove.

By the time Miguel emerged from the shower dressed in a clean pair of cutoffs, the table was set.

"I don't know how to light the stove," Bree told him.

"That's okay, I'll do it. You pour the wine." He looked at Bree and grinned. "Your Paris friends should see you now."

The shirt reached to her midthighs. She was barefoot and her face was rosy from the sun. He thought she'd never looked more beautiful. When they slid into the booth she looked at him over the glass of wine. "Cheers, Miguel."

"Cheers, Bree." He heard a deep-throated roll of thunder and felt the boat rock with a sudden hard slash of rain. She paused with her hand midair, her green eyes wide and her lips parted.

He covered her hand with his own. "It's all right, Bree," he told her. "We're going to ride this out just fine."

She took a deep breath. One bare foot touched his as though for reassurance and she summoned a smile. "Will we be able to get a message to Key West?"

Miguel nodded. "I'll do it as soon as we've finished." His toes covered hers. "I'm sorry, Bree. I should have checked the weather sooner."

"Is it a hurricane?"

"No, just a tropical storm that blew up out of nowhere. It'll calm down by morning."

She nodded and took a sip of her wine. She hadn't been afraid up on deck when it had been light, but it seemed different and more frightening now that darkness had descended. The boat lurched from side to side and the rain beat hard against the windows. Even though they lay close to the island, they were far away from civilization, alone and vulnerable here in the storm that seemed to grow worse every minute. She tried to eat and couldn't. Thunder shook the boat and she flinched.

"I'm going to call the ranger station." Miguel slid out of the booth. He knew the storm was getting to Bree and that he had to take her mind off it. Perhaps she'd feel better if he got word to her mother that they were safe.

He contacted the ranger station again and asked if they would relay a message to his father in Key West that they'd reached a safe harbor. When the station assured him they'd take care of it he turned back to Bree and said, "Dad will call your mother, Bree." He rested a hand on her shoulder. "We're going to be all right," he said. "The storm will pass by morning."

But the storm worried him more than he wanted to let on. The wind was stronger than it had been an hour ago and the sea was rougher. He could feel the boat turn and shift and that bothered him.

"I'm going to make sure everything is all right and battened down," he told Bree, trying to keep his growing concern out of his voice. He turned to leave, but because her eyes were wide with alarm he hesitated, then brusquely said, "Clean up in here, will you?" and ran up the stairs before she could object.

By the time Miguel returned, Bree had the galley in order. He looked around him in approval and said, "I think the wind's lessening a bit." He rested a hand on her shoulder. "We're both tired, Bree, let's try to get some rest."

Miguel wanted to make love to her but he wasn't sure it was what she wanted. He indicated the bunk and said, "That's pretty comfortable."

"Where will you..." Her tongue darted out to moisten one corner of her mouth. "What about you?"

"When I fold up the table and slide the cushions from the booth I have a bunk. It's comfortable enough to sleep one."

"I see." Bree looked at him, then away. "Well, then, I guess I'll..." She let the words hang in the air. The boat rocked suddenly, staggering her. She clutched at a wall that wasn't there and found herself skittering across the floor.

"Steady." Miguel reached her in one stride and put out his hands to her. "You okay?"

"Yes." Her voice sounded breathless. "I guess I haven't quite gotten my sea legs."

"I guess not." His hands tightened on her arms. He looked at her and it seemed to Bree that everything stood still. She tried to say his name but it came out as only a voiceless whisper before he gathered her in his arms.

His lips were firm, yet soft against hers. The arms that held her were strong. The kiss deepened, implored, demanded. Bree swayed against him. Clutching his shoulders for support, she felt the warmth of his skin against her open palm.

She didn't object when he began to unbutton the too-big shirt, so eager was she for the touch of his skin against hers. She gasped with pleasure when he pressed her close. Her breasts were soft against him, and the curly hairs on his chest tickled her delicate skin. She rubbed against him and felt him shudder.

With a smothered groan Miguel picked her up and carried her to the bunk. He laid her down and swiftly pulled the shirt off her shoulders and tossed it aside. When she was naked he looked at her for a moment. His face was tense, his dark eyes narrowed, his nostrils fluted with passion.

There was the sharp sound of the zipper as he removed his cutoffs. Then he was beside her, over her. His mouth captured hers, hot and insistent as his tongue prodded past her lips to the moistness of her mouth. He gasped with pleasure when her tongue danced to meet his.

Bree felt the strength of his masculinity against her leg and shivered with the knowledge of what was to come. She cupped his face in her hands, loving the roughness of his beard against her fingers. She traced the line of his brow, his cheekbones, then threaded her fingers through the thickness of his hair.

Suddenly Miguel captured her wrists and lifted them above her head so that her breasts were raised upward. "I love your breasts," he murmured as he flicked his tongue across first one, then the other, and when Bree quivered and whispered his name his body swelled with desire.

"You like that, don't you?" he asked.

"Miguel, please..." Her body quivered. "Yes," she said. "Oh, yes, yes, I like it."

He flicked her breasts again with his tongue, then took one nipple between his lips.

Bree moaned with pleasure and arched her body toward his hungry mouth—all thought, all reason lost in the bliss of the moment. Her body was on fire as it yearned toward his. She wanted him now, desperately wanted him to join his body to hers in a celebration of love.

But Miguel took his time, feeling a deep pleasure in the waiting—in knowing that he would soon thrust himself into her and feel her softness close around him.

Bree struggled to break free from the hand that held her wrists. She needed to touch him. Her body burned with desire. She couldn't bear this sweet agony a moment longer.

"Please," she whispered. "Oh, please, Miguel, let me go."

"In a minute, sweetheart." He continued kissing her breasts, teasing them with his tongue and his fingers.

Finally he released her and covered her mouth with his while she arched her body upward. "In a minute, *amor de mi vida*, in a minute."

He trailed a line of burning kisses down her body, across her naked belly. He moved lower and tightened his hands on her hips when she struggled.

"Sweet love," he whispered against her skin and kissed her so tenderly that his lips were only a whisper against her flesh.

A low whimpering sigh escaped her lips as she gave herself up to his hotly demanding passion that weakened and warmed and excited her to the point of madness. Suddenly she was on fire, writhing under the hands that held her as she whispered his name in a litany of wild desire. Then she cried out, a soft exultant cry that was lost in the keening of the wind.

Miguel lifted himself above her. He cupped her face with his hands and said, "Look at me, Bree. Look at me when I join my body to yours."

His body was fierce and strong against hers, awakening her again. He sought her mouth and kissed her with all the strength of his great passion. She wept for joy and in a surge of pleasure she lifted her body to his and cried out his name.

Together then, holding each other close, they tumbled off the edge of the world. As they clung together in those final thrilling moments of ecstasy he buried his face in her hair. He kissed her and told her how wonderful she was and that she belonged to him, for now, forever.

She clung to him, unable to speak, to tell him all that was in her heart. Her body felt free and alive, every pore, every fiber was awake and tingling with awareness. Then, as he stroked her, she relaxed and a wonderful somnolence settled upon her. She burrowed her face against his throat, loving the feel of him, the man scent of his skin.

"Miguel?" she whispered.

"Yes, love?"

"I've never..." She touched the side of his face. "I've never felt like this before—like the way you've made me feel."

Miguel tightened his arms around her as a surge of happiness flowed through his body. He wanted to tell her then that he loved her, that he had always loved her. But something held him back. Bree was his for the moment only. She was a dream that was too lovely to last and when the reunion was over she'd leave.

He kissed the top of her head, wondering how he could go on without her, with only the memory of her to last him through all the years of his life. The thought of losing her was too painful to bear. Perhaps he didn't have to lose her. Perhaps if he told her he loved her—if he asked her to stay and marry him— she would. Perhaps if he said the words...

"Bree?"

She snuggled against him sleepily. Then her breathing evened and he knew that now wasn't the time for words. "Sleep, my love," Miguel said into the darkness of the night.

Just before dawn the wind stilled and the sea became calm. The yacht moved quietly on the water, the waves lapping gently against her hull. Slowly, like a diver rising to the surface, Bree struggled up from the depths of a deep sleep. Her head rested on Miguel's shoulder, her arm circled his waist. She felt his hand, warm against her hip. She sighed, and when she did he slid it up to caress her breasts.

Without opening her eyes she murmured, "G'morning."

"Good morning." He kissed the top of her head, then tilting her face up, kissed her closed eyelids, her nose and finally her mouth.

A lovely warmth flooded through Bree as suddenly every nerve end began to tingle with awareness. She answered Miguel's kiss and moved closer, and when he bent to kiss her breasts she cradled his head in the hollow of her shoulder. With closed eyes she gave herself up to all of the pleasurable sensations coursing through her body, the warmth of his lips against her flesh, the silkiness of the hair she spread her fingers through.

When finally he joined his body to hers she rose to meet him, more confident now of her own responses. She turned her face, seeking the mouth she loved, losing herself in the kiss and in the surge of feeling that shook her to the very depths of her being.

At last, still close and clinging, still in the throes of passion, Bree whispered, "What a wonderful way to awaken. I'd like..." She hesitated. She wanted to tell him that she'd like to awaken this way every morning for the rest of her life. But she didn't want Miguel to think that because they'd made love she expected him to make a commitment.

"You'd like what?" His arms tightened around her.

"A great, huge breakfast." She forced a smile. "All this fresh air and exercise..." She blushed. "You know what I mean."

"Yes, I know what you mean." He swung his legs out of the bunk, trying to hide a vague feeling of disappointment. "Why don't you rustle us up some breakfast while I go topside and check on the boat? There's ham in the refrigerator and waffles in the freezer."

Bree watched him pull his cut-offs up over his legs and hurry up to the deck. She stood in the center of the cabin for a moment, then with a sigh she dressed in her shorts and T-shirt and began to prepare breakfast. She was learning how to manage in this galley kitchen and found that it was fun to cook in a smaller space than she was used to.

As she worked she found herself thinking what a pleasure it would be to set sail on a longer trip—maybe for a week or a month—to live like this, day after day, with Miguel. Mentally she stocked the cupboards with the basics. She didn't know about fresh fruits and vegetables but she assumed they'd be able to buy those things in ports along the way.

They'd sail to Nassau, then on to Eleuthera. Maybe on down the Antilles to Antigua, Dominica, Martinique and St. Lucia, taking the time to luxuriate in this wondrous thing that was happening between them.

She looked down at the ham sizzling in the pan and wondered what it would be like to spend so many sun-filled, lazy days with Miguel. To go to sleep in his arms at night, to awaken to his kisses each morning.

Bree shook her head and tried to bring herself back to reality. She was letting her imagination run away with her just because she'd spent a night with Miguel. She had her work to think about and Miguel had his—thousands of miles away from Paris.

She smiled. Her friend of long ago had turned into one of the best looking, most exciting men she'd ever known. She'd never experienced, had never hoped to experience, what she and Miguel had shared yesterday and last night.

He was a wonderful, gentle lover. In the few hours they'd shared she felt closer to him than she'd ever felt to anybody in her life. He'd been a friend first, then a lover. She didn't know how she could bear to leave him.

When they'd eaten they took their coffee and went up on deck to a world washed clean by wind and rain. The sea, an unbelievable shade of turquoise green, was so clear they could see down to the depths of the sandy bottom. The walls of Fort Jefferson reflected the sunlight.

"We should start back," Miguel said at last.

"I know. My mother must be frantic."

"I'm sure the marine radio got through to Dad. He would have called her."

"But she'll be nervous until I'm actually in Key West." Bree smiled. "My mother and I have had our differences, Miguel, but I've never doubted how much she loves me." Bree hesitated. "I'm sorry she and your dad don't get along."

"He's pretty good-humored about it, Bree. Every time he goes to a council meeting he says he's off to do battle with his nemesis. But I think maybe he enjoys it. He said once that your mother was a worthy adversary, that if she thought she was right she'd stick to her guns no matter what. 'Come hellfire, flood or damnation,' he told me once, 'Cornelia Petersen will fight for what she believes in right down to the wire.'" Miguel grinned. "My father may not get along with her, but I have a hunch he thinks she's one hell of a woman."

One hell of a woman? Bree smiled inwardly, wondering what her mother would think of that description.

In a little while Miguel hoisted the sails and headed back toward the Florida coast. Because of the storm there were only a few boats out on the water and it seemed almost as though they were alone on the vast ocean. At noontime Miguel put in to a small, deserted island. Sliding the boat in among an overhang of seagrape trees, he said, "How about a swim before lunch?"

Bree nodded as she pushed her sweat-damp hair back off her face. "Yes, I'd like that. I'll go below and put my suit on."

But as she turned away Miguel put a restraining hand on her arm. "There's no need to do that," he said.

Bree looked at him and a flush crept into her cheeks. She took a deep breath and slowly nodded.

Miguel watched her, his lower lip caught between strong white teeth while she pulled the T-shirt over her head and stepped out of her shorts. He knew what this cost her. He saw the downcast eyes, the flush of color in her cheeks. And his body swelled with longing and with pride because she was doing this for him.

He stepped close to her and putting a finger under her chin raised her face and gently brushed her lips with his.

Once again he wanted to tell her he loved her. And once again something held him back.

The water was cool on their bodies. They swam together in the secluded pool, then hand in hand floated on their backs, feeling the sun on their naked bodies.

"I've never felt so free," she said. "It's as though I'm a part of all this. As though you and I are the only ones left in the world."

"That's the way I feel sometimes when I'm sailing alone. It's a good feeling, isn't it?" He let his body sink down into the water and coming up beside her said, "But I don't think I ever want to sail alone again, Bree."

"Miguel . . . ?"

"No, don't say anything." He covered her mouth with his. His arms and his legs encircled her body.

She was lost in him, floating free in the turquoise water, clinging to him as though she'd never let him go. Now it was Bree who sought his mouth, who kissed him with fervor, trying to tell him with her body all of the things she couldn't say in words.

Until at last Miguel held her away from him breathlessly. With a low moan of need he grasped her hips and joined his body to hers with a force that made her gasp aloud. He moved his hands around to her buttocks to hold her tight against him as together they slipped beneath the water.

Her eyes were opened when he kissed her and her long blond hair floated behind her. He held her close, imprisoning her with his legs as he thrust fast and fiercely against her.

Suddenly he pulled away from her, so wild with passion that it shook him to the very roots of his being.

Breathlessly they surfaced. Miguel looked into the green eyes that were still hooded with desire. He put a hand against the back of her head and brought her close to him. An urgency filled him and taking her hand, he led her toward the boat.

When they were aboard he carried Bree down the stairs to the bunk.

"Let me dry..." she started to say. But Miguel shook his head. He needed her—wanted her now. Like a man who has gone without food too long he still hungered. He put his arms around her. "I don't know what you do to me, Bree," he said with a voice that shook with feeling. "I'm intoxicated by you. I don't think I'll ever get enough." He put his arms around her and pressed her slick wet body to his and rested the side of his face against her cheek.

She touched his sea-damp hair, then slid her hands down over his shoulders to his back. Tenderly they curved over the swell of his buttocks and when she felt the shape of his masculinity against her body she pressed him closer.

He kissed her then, kissed her with all the love and the passion of his body as he pressed her down on the bunk. He looked at her, his eyes dark with passion, and without a word joined his body to hers.

It was wild and impassioned. He moved quickly, deeply and fiercely against her, gasping his pleasure when with a glad cry Bree lifted her body to his.

Nothing, nothing would ever be this good again. Bree wanted to tell him that she loved him but she held back, afraid that her words might change this wonderful magic that was happening between them now. Afraid that if she said the words he'd pull away.

He moved deeply inside of her, taking her with a hunger that matched her own. Until it was too much—the passion past bearing. She almost cried aloud because she wanted this to last, but when she tried to hold back Miguel wouldn't let her. He raced on, taking her to the edge of sanity until helpless with desire, her body on fire with need, she clasped his shoulders and cried his name.

Miguel sought her lips. He took her words of passion into his mouth. Then his own body exploded and together they soared to a height neither of them had ever known before.

Chapter Seven

Miguel had never been happier in his life. These past years had been fulfilling in many ways—he'd made a success of a business that he enjoyed and more money than he'd ever need. He'd built the house he'd always dreamed of and he'd become a respected member of the community. Now it seemed to him that those things meant little after all. He hadn't known until yesterday what true happiness was. He'd never before experienced what he'd shared with Bree.

A little while ago, they'd made love with a passion that threatened to consume them. He'd been demanding, but when, aware of her fragility, he'd tried to hold back, she'd clung to him with an urgency that matched his own. She'd lifted her body to his and when at last he'd taken her cry into his mouth it had been with a joy unlike anything he'd ever experienced.

He loved her. He allowed himself to actually think the words. He loved Bree and he'd loved her since that night so long ago when, dressed in her prom finery, she'd come slowly toward him down the stairs.

He'd been hurt and angry that night when he'd seen her kissing Craig. Later, wanting to vent his rage, he'd taken her down to the beach. He wasn't sure, even now, what he'd planned to do that night. He only knew that when they knelt together on the sand and her body had trembled against his, he'd found that he could never do anything to hurt her.

But he'd left Key West because he'd been afraid to fight for Bree's love. He'd been young and foolish, but he wouldn't be foolish again. He wanted Bree and he wouldn't let anything stand in the way of having her.

Miguel's hand tightened on the tiller as he looked at her. The sun shone on her face, her marvelous hair blew free in the wind. She turned and smiled at him and heaven was in her eyes.

"Let's not go back to the reunion." He hadn't meant to say the words aloud, but now that they were out he was glad he'd spoken them. "Let's check out of the Beachcomber," he went on in a rush. "Hurricane season is almost over and as soon as it blows itself out, the weather'll be good. I'll take a couple of weeks off, maybe three. We'll lay in some supplies and set sail to anywhere you want to go."

Bree stared at Miguel. It was as though he'd looked into the thoughts she'd had this morning about stocking up and sailing to... to anywhere. She closed her eyes and hugging her knees thought what it would be like. Sailing, swimming off the side of the boat, fixing meals in the small galley. Making love to Miguel to the slow roll of the boat beneath them. It was a dream, but it wasn't reality.

"I can't," Bree said. "My job..." She shook her head. "I'm only going to be in Key West for a few days after the reunion." She tried to smile. "My mother'd have apoplexy."

"You're thirty-three years old."

"I know, but..." Not quite meeting his eyes, Bree continued, "She's very old-fashioned about things like that."

Too afraid now to tell her that he loved her, Miguel hesitated, then said, "I care about you."

"And I care about you."

"But?"

"Everything's happened so fast, Miguel. We need time."

"A cruise would give us that time," he said urgently. "I want to be with you, Bree. I want to spend lazy days in the sun with you, loving you. I want to sleep with you and wake up with you." His voice was low, intense. "I want time for both of us to get to know each other again."

"I promised Dawn I'd help her through the reunion."

"It'll be over on Sunday night. If the hurricane's moved up the coast we could leave by Tuesday or Wednesday."

Bree hesitated, not knowing how to explain to him how important her career was to her. "I can't take that much time off, Miguel. I have to be back in Paris before the end of the month and I have to stop in New York first. I can't..." She tried to smile. "I can't just sail off into the sunset."

"Can't you?" His eyes were bleak. He looked at Bree, then away, out over the foam-crested waves. "No, I don't suppose you can."

End of dream. End of thinking what had happened between them meant as much to Bree as it meant to him. It obviously hadn't. This had been a nice romantic idyll for her, nothing more.

They spoke little as the hours passed. Once he asked her to take the tiller while he went below to contact his father on the marine radio. Bree heard him tell Antonio that they should be in Key West in about two hours. His father sounded worried when he asked if Bree was all right.

Was she all right? Bree rested her elbows on her knees as she gazed out over the water. It seemed impossible that she and Miguel had only been gone for a day and a half. So much had happened in that short space of time—enough to change her life.

But Bree wasn't sure she wanted her life changed. She was happy—she'd *been* happy—with what she had, a lovely apartment overlooking The Tuileries, work that she loved and took pride in and a circle of friends that she enjoyed.

A few years ago, she'd put the thought of marriage and children somewhere on the back burner of her mind. Now the thought of a child, a child who would look like Miguel, made her heart leap with longing.

Bree closed her eyes. She knew she was letting her thoughts get ahead of herself. Miguel hadn't said anything about marriage, he'd only suggested a two- or three-week cruise. It would be wonderful, but... Her sigh was painful. But that wasn't reality. Miguel had to understand that she, too, had responsibilities and that she had to go back to Paris when the reunion was over.

As they neared the Key West marina they saw two figures at the end of the dock. "That's Dad," Miguel said. He narrowed his eyes against the glare of the sun. "I think that's your mother with him." He turned to Bree. "Unless I miss my guess my dad's going to give me hell and your mother's going to tear me limb from limb. She's got both hands on her hips and she looks like she's ready to do battle."

Cornelia was indeed ready to do battle. She glared out the approaching yawl, then glared at Antonio Rivas, sure that in some way this was all his fault because it was his son who'd taken Bree out on his boat in hurricane weather.

She'd almost fainted when she heard Antonio Rivas's voice on the telephone. He'd tried to tell her that everything would be all right, but she'd started to cry. Antonio had waited for her to get under control, then he'd comforted her with soothing words—telling her to rest.

But Cornelia hadn't rested. She'd never been as frightened in her life. She'd only been able to think of her grandfather Alex, whose fishing boat had gone down near the Tortugas in a storm just like the one that Bree was in. She knew how vast the ocean was, how capricious and dangerous. She thought of the angry, roiling waves crashing over the bow of the yawl, of Bree washed over the side, and she'd gone down on her knees in desperate, wordless prayer.

She'd paced the parlor. She'd drunk endless cups of strong black tea, and finally, with a framed photograph of Bree on her lap, she'd gone to sleep in the rocker.

Now she stood at the end of the dock beside Antonio Rivas, clutching her purse to her breast.

"*Hola,*" Antonio cried when the boat drew closer. "Are you and Bree all right?"

"Yes, Dad, we're fine." Miguel tossed out the mooring rope. His father caught and secured it, then reached down to help Bree up to the dock. "Are you all right, *muchacha*?" he asked.

"Yes, Antonio. Thanks."

Miguel jumped up to the dock beside her and his father embraced him. Pounding Miguel's back he said, "*Dios,* Miguel, you had us worried. I prayed to every saint in heaven for your safety." He put an arm around Bree's shoulders and gave her a bear hug.

Bree cast a worried glance at her mother. She put her arm around Cornelia and said, "I know how worried you must have been. I'm sorry."

"It wasn't your fault." Cornelia clasped Bree close. She glared at Miguel over Bree's shoulder. "It was his."

"No, mother." Bree stepped back. "The storm came up without any warning. There wasn't anything Miguel could do."

"He's used to boats." Cornelia glared at him. "What you did, taking Bree out when a storm was brewing, is inexcusable and irresponsible. Weren't you listening to the marine radio? What were you doing? What was the matter with you?" Cornelia's face was flushed with anger. She pressed her fingers to her lips, unable to go on.

"Take it easy, Mrs. Petersen," Antonio said. "The storm came up out of nowhere. It wasn't Miguel's fault. He—"

"But it was my fault." Miguel stepped up to Cornelia. "I'm very sorry," he said. "I know how worried you must have been, Mrs. Petersen."

"I doubt that you do," Cornelia said coldly. "Now if you'll excuse us, I'd like to take my daughter home."

"But I'm staying at the hotel, Mother," Bree protested.

"I don't care where you're staying," Cornelia said waspishly. "You're coming home for a bath and some decent food. There's nothing special going on with the reunion tonight. You can go back to the hotel later if you want to."

Cornelia held her hand out to Antonio. "Thank you for telephoning me, Mr. Rivas." She glared at Miguel as she said, "Now come along, Bree."

Bree didn't want to leave Miguel, not this way, but she understood that her mother had been terribly worried and that Cornelia needed her at home right now. She put her hand on Miguel's arm. "Thank you for getting me safely through the storm," she said. "I'll...I'll be in touch." She knew that the words sounded inane and inadequate after all that had passed between them.

Bree went home with her mother. She bathed and ate the meal her mother had prepared, not even complaining when Cornelia placed a second helping on her plate. Finally she went up to her room to rest. She slept for a few hours and awoke thinking of Miguel, knowing she had to talk to him. She couldn't leave the discussion they'd had earlier today on the boat hanging in the air. She'd seen his expression when she'd told him she couldn't go away with him; the fleeting look of hurt before he'd turned away. She had to see him, she had to explain.

Cornelia was sitting on the front porch when Bree came downstairs. Bree took the wicker rocking chair next to her mother. "This is my favorite time of the day," she said, "when everything seems so still." She gazed out over the well-kept lawn. "Wherever I go," she murmured, "this will always be home." She reached for her mother's hand. "I'm so sorry you were worried."

Cornelia took a long painful breath. "I'd have died if anything had happened to you." She swallowed hard and glancing sideways at Bree, said, "What happened last night?"

"We..." Bree felt hot color creep into her cheeks. "The storm came up suddenly," she said. "We made it to Fort Jefferson and Miguel found a place on the lee side of the island that was sheltered from the wind. We rode the storm out there. This morning the wind had died and it was almost as though it had been calm for days."

"I see."

There was no sound except for the agitated rocking of Cornelia's chair until she said, "I'll go fetch us some key lime pie."

Bree didn't want a piece of pie but she was so relieved that her mother had changed the subject that she didn't protest when Cornelia returned with two large slices. She finished hers and said, "I'd better get back to the Beachcomber, Mother. Dawn said yesterday that the committee would get together for a meeting some time today."

Cornelia sighed. "Then I guess you'd better run along." She smoothed her dress, then stood and put the two plates on the porch railing. "Get to bed early tonight," she said. "You've been through a bad experience; you need your rest."

Bree put her arms around her mother. "I will," she said. "You go to bed early, too. I don't imagine you had much sleep last night."

"Not much." Cornelia walked Bree out to the rental car. "You drive carefully, hear?"

"I will." She kissed her mother's cheek. "I'll call you in the morning," she said.

Bree drove down toward the beach, but at the corner of Duval and Caroline Street she hesitated. Then, instead of turning in the direction of the Beachcomber she turned north.

Two miles out she found the narrow lane leading to Miguel's beach home. She tightened her hands on the steering wheel. She wasn't sure that she should do this, she only knew she couldn't wait until tomorrow to see Miguel.

He'd built the house on a rise of land overlooking the sea. A sprawling one-story structure, made of fine wood and stone, it was surrounded by live oaks, Australian pines and royal palms.

Bree pulled into the driveway, hesitant now that she was there. She left the car, went up to the front door and rang the bell. When there was no response, she followed a graveled path around the side of the house. A two-car garage stood open with a car and a pickup parked inside. She hesitated, then opened the gate that led to the back. As she rounded the corner of the house, she gasped.

The view in the approaching darkness was breathtaking. The sea, like the sky, had turned golden in the last rays of the sun. There was nothing on the horizon as far as she could see except for the gulls and pelicans that swooped low over a school of fish, and a family of sandpipers strutting on the beach below. Seagrape trees, flame-colored hibiscus and sago palms surrounded the wide patio. The air was filled with the sweet scent of night-blooming jasmine.

"Good evening."

Startled, Bree looked around. Miguel, a glass of white wine in one hand, was reclining in a bubbling hot tub that was partially hidden from view by ferns and potted azaleas.

"Good . . . good evening," Bree managed.

"I'm sorry. I didn't know you were coming. I would have dressed."

"No, that's all right. I looked up the address in the phone book."

Miguel nodded. Indicating the tub he asked, "Would you like to come in? The water's fine."

"No, no thank you."

"Then I'll come out." Miguel put the glass down and stepped out of the tub.

Drops of water glistened on his naked body. He stood for a moment, his skin bronzed in the sunset, tall and lean and hard. His wide shoulders tapered down to his narrow waist and hips, and long perfect legs. Unself-consciously he reached for a towel and wrapped it around his waist.

Bree moistened her lips. Somewhere in her midsection she felt a tiny spark catch fire. He was so handsome as he stood there, his body outlined against the afterglow of the sun.

In a voice she scarcely recognized as her own she said, "You have a wonderful view of the ocean."

Miguel nodded. "You should see it in the morning." One eyebrow lifted and with a slight smile he added, "Any morning you'd like. I'll order a special sunrise just for you. Come in, I'll show you the rest of the house."

He led the way across the flagstone patio and opening a screen door, led her into the living room and switched on a light. "Make yourself comfortable," he said. "I'll be right back."

It was a man's room, all browns and golds and beiges. There were two soft leather sofas and recliners that faced the floor-to-ceiling windows looking out over the water, end tables and a big driftwood coffee table with sailing magazines scattered on top of it. Bookcases covered one wall and there was a large stone fireplace on the opposite side of the room.

Above the fireplace there were a series of framed photographs. As Bree moved closer she saw they were *her* photographs and her eyes widened with surprise.

Two of them were black-and-white sea pictures she'd taken when she was fifteen and just learning to use a camera. They weren't bad, she thought as she studied them. There was a feeling about them that showed her love of the sea even though they weren't technically perfect.

The three photographs that were in color had been clipped from different issues of *Our World Magazine*. One was of novitiate nuns she'd spotted one day in Montparnasse. They'd been clustered in a group, chattering like a flock of young blackbirds. As she raised her camera they stopped to look in a store window at the spring fashions they'd never wear. There'd been the shadow of sadness in their young eyes, the barest suppressed hint of longing. By pure luck, she'd captured that sudden show of emotion with her camera.

Another photo was one she'd taken in Greece just after an earthquake. The third was from a series she'd done of Provence in the spring.

The last photograph was one that Miguel had taken of her, with her camera, during their senior year at high school. She was dressed in blue jeans that were rolled to mid-calf and an old blue shirt. She was barefoot. Her toes were digging into the sand and her hair was wind-tousled around her face. She was laughing into the camera.

"That's the way I like to remember you," Miguel said as he came up beside her.

"I can't remember ever being that young." Bree turned to look at him. She was surprised that Miguel had followed her work, and touched that he'd kept the copies of her very first attempts, and that funny wind-blown picture of her.

He rested his hands on his shoulders. "You were an awfully pretty kid, Bree."

"Was I?" She stared at the picture of herself with a puzzled frown. "I never thought of myself as pretty, Miguel. I always felt too tall and thin, too... you know."

He shook his head. "No, I don't know. To me you were the prettiest girl in Key West." His hands tightened. "You were pretty then—you're beautiful now."

She wanted to tell him that that was how he made her feel. She'd never known how he'd felt all these years—that he cared about her. Why else would he have kept her photographs?

But Bree didn't say any of the things that were in her heart. Instead she let Miguel take her hand and lead her to the sofa.

"Would you like a glass of wine?" he said.

"Yes, please." Bree paused to looked around her. "This is a lovely room, Miguel."

"Thanks." He went to a built-in bar next to the fireplace and when he'd poured white wine into a tulip glass, he came to the sofa and looking down at her said, "I'm glad you're here, Bree."

"I had to come. I wanted to tell you how sorry I was for what my mother said this afternoon."

"She was right. What happened *was* inexcusable and irresponsible. I should have been listening to the marine radio. Instead..," Miguel sank down to the sofa beside Bree. "Instead, I got lost in you," he said quietly. "When I touched you...the first time we made love..." He took the wineglass from her hand. "Tell me the real reason you came here tonight."

Bree was afraid her heart would leap from her body. She was sure Miguel could hear its thunderous beating. She looked into his eyes and saw the warmth there, the desire, and she, too, was lost. He clasped her hand in his and it was as though he'd seared her flesh. He stood up and pulling her close whispered, "Come with me, Bree."

He led her to his bedroom. He turned off the air-conditioning and pulling back the drapes, he opened the French doors so they could hear the deep roll of the sea. He yanked off his T-shirt and stepped out of his trousers. When he stood naked beside her he said, "Let me undress you, Bree."

With fingers that shook with need, Miguel unfastened the buttons of her dress and slipped it over her head. He stood for a moment looking at her before he reached around her back and unfastened the lacy yellow bra. Then he picked her up and carried her to the big bed in the center of the room.

He held her for a moment, breathing in the scent of her before he laid her down and removed her sandals. He looked down at her, drinking in the loveliness of her body, then eased the wisp of yellow satin down over her hips.

He switched on the bedside lamp and tilted the shade so that the soft glow reflected on the curves of her body. Placing one knee on the bed he covered her breast with his hand. "This is why you came," he said.

"Yes," Bree whispered. "This is why I came."

"I want to make love to you." He brushed the fair hair back from her face and gently kissed her lips. "Like I did that night on the boat, Bree. I want to feel you tremble against me. I want to hear you whisper my name when I join my body to yours. I want . . ."

Miguel buried his face against her throat. He longed to tell her that he wanted to believe that tonight she belonged to him—and that she loved him as much as he loved her.

She did belong to him, for now, for this brief time they were together. As he belonged to her.

Bree looked up at him. She touched his cheek, then slid one hand around the back of his neck and brought his face down to hers. He kissed her again and gathered her in his arms so that he could feel the whole silken length of her against his naked body. Tonight she was his.

She melted against him, trembling with the sureness of what was to come. She parted her lips and when her tongue danced against his, a flame of desire sparked between them. She threaded her fingers through his hair, holding him close, wanting this kiss to go on forever.

Miguel took his time, sampling her lips, drinking in the taste of her, nibbling the corners of her mouth. He rained kisses over her face, her eyelids, her nose, her cheeks, down to her shell-pink ears. His teeth fastened on one dainty earlobe and he felt her shiver with pleasure.

"Miguel," she said against his shoulder. "Ah, Miguel, I love . . . I love what you do to me."

His hands were warm against her body. He touched her breasts and she lifted her arms to encircle his shoulders. "No, Bree. Just let me pleasure you," he said softly.

She closed her eyes and gave herself up to the lovely warmth that flooded her body as he caressed her. He touched her breasts with magical fingers, holding them with gentle hands, kissing them so tenderly she wanted to weep.

"You're so beautiful," he said as he moved his hands down her body. "Your skin is so soft, so pale." He brushed gentle kisses across her stomach and when she shivered with pleasure he moved around to her hips, licking her as a cat would lick her kittens. Everywhere he touched, her skin caught fire. Unable to hold back, she whispered his name, and when he parted her legs she writhed against him.

His strong hands soothed her to calmness. He rested his face against her stomach for a moment, then with the utmost tenderness bent to kiss her thighs. "Sweet love," he crooned against her skin. "Oh, my sweet love."

He kissed her until Bree thought she would surely die of pleasure. When her body began to tremble he said, "Wait, darling, wait for me," and slipped inside her.

It would never be like this again, Bree thought as she clung to him. Every time they made love that thought was present, but this time... No, nothing would ever be this good again. She yearned toward him, whimpering small cries of joy, telling him how good this was, how she loved what he did to her.

Bree was almost out of control. At this moment in time nothing else mattered but Miguel. She wanted to be a part of him—of his flesh, of the heart and soul of him. She wanted to tell him, tried to tell him. But her body was on fire, reaching for release as he carried her higher and higher on a crest of passion she hadn't thought possible.

She heard the rasp of breath in his throat, his sharp cries of pleasure, and thought her heart would burst with love.

Miguel murmured her name as he wrapped his arms around her to hold her closer, to rock her to him.

His cadence was the cadence of the sea, surging in and out, each surge stronger than the next. Until that final crashing crest of ecstasy that flung them, shattered and breathless, onto the shore.

She rested against him and whispered his name. Tears streaked her face; her body still shook with passion.

"Bree," Miguel murmured against her hair. "Oh, Bree, do you know what you do to me? Do you have any idea how you make me feel?"

Miguel stopped himself from saying his words of love. He wanted to beg her to marry him but he was afraid—this was only a dream and dreams never really came true.

Miguel kissed the top of her head. How would he ever live without her? he asked himself. Filled with his love for her he rocked her gently until she slept.

But he didn't sleep. He only listened to the waves breaking against the shore. And held her and kissed her while he silently told her all the things that were in his heart.

Chapter Eight

It was a little before midnight when they drove back to the hotel. Miguel walked Bree to her room, kissed her good-night and told her that he would see her at the banquet.

It had been a long day and Bree was tired, but when she got into bed and closed her eyes, she found the bed curiously empty. She told herself that was ridiculous, that she'd slept alone all her life, but it didn't help. She missed the warmth of Miguel next to her, his slow steady breathing, the hand that reached for hers even when he slept.

Bree lay awake for a long time. Even when she finally slept, she reached out for Miguel, murmuring a protest in her sleep because he wasn't beside her. In the morning when she awoke she lay for a long time staring up at the ceiling, wondering how she could have gotten so used to being with Miguel in such a short space of time. She'd missed him last night with an intensity that was almost a physical ache.

Be careful, Bree told herself. The last few days had been wonderful, but Miguel hadn't spoken about anything more permanent than a vacation together. She sighed and closed her eyes and an expression very akin to pain crossed her face. Even if Miguel had said anything about permanency, she would have had to back away. Despite their present feelings, there were too many aspects of their lives that kept them apart.

But that didn't mean she and Miguel couldn't be friends. Well...more than friends. Perhaps she'd be able to fly back to Florida for Christmas; maybe Miguel could come to Paris next summer.

Feeling oddly defeated, Bree got out of bed. The phone rang just before she got in the shower. It was Dawn. "Bad news," she told Bree. "Hurricane Lola has veered toward Cuba. If she keeps heading in the same direction, she'll hit us."

Bree's hand tightened on the phone. "When?"

"Maybe by tomorrow night." Dawn groaned. "Just in time for the dance!"

"What are we going to do?"

"Go on just as we've planned, I suppose. It's still too early to tell exactly what course the storm will take. The weather bureau is hedging, saying maybe it'll head out to open sea, which would be fine."

"Except for the boats that are out there—the shrimpers."

"Yeah." Dawn's sigh was audible. "This is one of the joys of living in Florida, Bree. You just never know. I'm hoping it'll poop out. In the meantime we'll go ahead with everything as though Lola didn't exist. Are you ready for breakfast?"

"I will be in about thirty minutes. Shall I meet you downstairs?"

"Yes. Jean, Gwen and Carris are joining us so we can talk about the banquet tonight." There was a pause, then Dawn said, "I heard you and Miguel ran into a storm. I was really worried, Bree. We all were. I called your mother when you didn't come back and she was frantic. She called me as soon as she got word you and Miguel were all right." Dawn hesitated. Carefully she said, "Your mother said you were heading for the Tortugas. Is that where you rode the storm out?"

"Yes. We anchored on the lee side of Fort Jefferson."

"All night?"

"Uh-huh." Bree cleared her throat. "Look, I'd better get in the shower."

"Sure, okay."

Bree waited, bracing herself for more questions.

"I like Miguel. He's a great guy, Bree. You make a good-looking couple." When Bree didn't answer, Dawn said, "Well, I . . . I'll see you downstairs."

Bree stared at the phone after she'd hung up, wondering how many other people knew that she and Miguel had spent the night on his boat. As she pulled the nightgown over her head she breathed a silent prayer that Gwen wasn't one of them.

So much for unanswered prayers. When Bree sat down at one of the tables on the patio thirty minutes later, Gwen arched a thinly penciled brow and said, "I heard about your little adventure on the high seas, Bree dear. How exciting! To think that you and Miguel had to spend the night together on the boat." She leaned across the table. "I had no idea there was anything between the two of you." She looked at the others at the table and with a laugh said, "If there wasn't anything before I dare say there is now."

"You used to go together in high school, didn't you?" Jean asked.

"No, Jean." Bree trying hard to be patient. "Miguel and I were just friends in high school."

"But you went to the prom with him." Gwen propped her elbows on the table and to Jean said, "Don't you remember? Bree had a crush on Craig. When he didn't ask her to the prom she settled for Miguel and Craig went with Bobbie Lee." Gwen began to butter a roll. "Poor Bobbie Lee," she said. "Craig would have done much better with you, Bree."

"My God!" Carris shook his head. "Is this what women talk about when they get together? I thought we were here to discuss the banquet tonight."

"We are," Dawn said firmly. She glared at Gwen and looking down at the yellow pad beside her plate said, "All right, let's get started."

"What about the hurricane?" Carris asked.

"I checked with the weather bureau just before I left my room," Dawn said. "They're pretty sure the storm will hit Cuba, then it's anybody's guess."

"What do we do if it heads in this direction?" Jean looked concerned. "Do you think we ought to call off the dance tomorrow night?"

"I'm not sure. We'll have to make that decision tomorrow morning, I suppose. We're all staying here at the hotel and when we know more we'll call everybody together and decide what we're going to do." Dawn glanced at her watch. "Bree and I have to meet Frannie and Eleanor in fifteen minutes." She finished her coffee and pushed her chair back. "Ready, Bree?"

This was the first Bree had heard of a meeting with Frannie and Eleanor, but she nodded and got up. Only when they were out of earshot of the others did she say, "I didn't know anything about a meeting."

"I didn't mention it because you don't really have to be there. The alternative is putting up with more of Gwen's questions."

Bree grinned at her friend. "Then lead on. I'm all yours."

Dawn looked at her. "I guess you know I'm curious about you and Miguel, don't you? I don't suppose you want to tell me what's happening between the two of you?"

Bree hesitated. "I'm not sure what's happening, Dawn. But whatever it is it's happened so fast my head is spinning." She linked her arm with Dawn's. "I keep telling myself that Miguel and I are just good friends and that I'm only here for a couple of weeks, but..." She shook her head. "I've never felt this way before, Dawn—not about anyone—and I guess the feeling scares me. I don't want to say anything more right now because I'm so mixed up I'm not even making sense."

"Okay, Bree, just remember that I'm here whenever you want to talk. Come on, let's go to that meeting."

It was a day of meetings and of speculation about the course Hurricane Lola would take. By late afternoon the storm had hit Cuba with one-hundred-and-thirty-five-mile-an-hour winds. The forecast for Florida looked bleak.

"Let's go ahead with the banquet tonight," Dawn said. "We can make an announcement there that we're putting the dance off until Sunday night. By then we'll know if we can go ahead with it or if we have to head for higher ground."

"We haven't had a really bad storm in years," Eleanor said.

"But the ones that hit us usually hit Cuba first." Dawn looked worried. "I have a bad feeling about old Lola. I think she's going to hit the Keys. I think she's going to knock the hell out of us."

"You always were a pessimist, Dawn." Frannie gave a nervous laugh. "I drove all the way to Miami to buy a dress for the dance and I'm darn well going to wear it."

"In my opinion we should cancel both the banquet and the dance and head for Miami," Jean said. "This really is a terrible storm. Winds up to a hundred and thirty-five miles an hour! It could blow us right off the map."

"It's not going to blow us off the map," Dawn said patiently. "We'll take every precaution we can and if we have to we'll cancel the dance." She glanced at her watch. "It's almost four. Let's call it a day. See you in the Neptune Room at seven forty-five."

They said their goodbyes then. The others headed into town to shop but Bree went up to her room. With a sigh she closed her door, thinking what a relief it was to be alone. She kicked her shoes off and crossing the room to the sliding doors of the balcony, opened them and breathed in the salt-sea air, a relief after being cooped up all day in air-conditioning. She stood for a moment looking out at the sea, then crossed back into the room just as the telephone rang.

"I've been trying to get to a phone all day," Miguel said. "I guess you've heard about the hurricane?"

"Yes." Bree sat down on the bed. "Is it still ripping through Cuba?"

"Yeah. Knocking the hell out of Mantanzas Province right about now."

"Do you think it'll hit the Keys?"

"It's anybody's guess at this point, Bree. It could still veer over to Andros or Eleuthera or even on up the coast to the Carolinas. But we've got to be prepared. Dad and I have spent the day trying to get our boats to a safe harbor. We've contacted all but three of them and we're still securing the boats in dock. I doubt that I'll be able to make it to the banquet but I will if I can. If I can't make it I'll catch up with you later." He hesitated. "Keep a light in the window for me."

"I will, Miguel."

"If the storm does hit I want you out of the hotel."

"But nothing's ever happened to the Beachcomber," Bree protested. "It's been here for over a hundred years."

"This is a killer storm, Bree. I won't let you take any chances. The Beachcomber's right on the beach, not built above it the way my home is. If Lola hits I want you out of there."

"And I don't want you anywhere around the docks if it hits," Bree said. "You get to higher ground where it's safe."

"We'll both get to higher ground. I've got to go now, Bree. There's a lot of work to do. I'll catch up with you sometime tonight."

"All right, Miguel. Take care."

Bree put the phone down. "I love you," she said aloud.

* * *

The cocktail party started with a flourish. A few of the alumni who hadn't been able to arrive in Key West in time for the reception were there. Bree discovered that Herbert Ellis, the quietest boy in the class of '72, had become an astronaut, and that George Lorringer, one of the few blacks in the class, was a lieutenant colonel in the army.

Red-haired Nancy Saunders, the most sought after girl in the class, was married to an insurance salesman and the mother of seven children. Teddy Jaboly, who'd been voted most likely to succeed, had a job parking cars in Miami.

Bobbie Lee sat at a table with the other members of the cheerleading squad and cast painful glances at Craig—which he ignored.

Even though Dawn had insisted the banquet start promptly at eight, it was hard to break up the groups chatting near the bar. Finally, at eight forty-five, Dawn clapped her hands and said, "On to the banquet, friends, before we're all too pixilated to find our plates."

With good-natured protests everybody headed for the tables. Everybody except Craig Logan. As the others turned away he grabbed Bree's hand. "Let's have one for the road," he coaxed. His voice was slurred, his steps unsteady.

"It's a mighty short road, Craig." Pulling him along with her, Bree headed in the direction of the banquet. He held back and speaking as patiently as she could she said, "They'll be serving wine with dinner. Come on, let's find a table."

"Will you sit with me, Bree? I'll come if you sit with me."

Bree frowned. She was distressed by Craig's drinking and uncomfortable with him. But rather than have him make a scene she let him take her arm and lead her to a table.

Before he sat down he turned to her. "And you'll have a drink with me when the banquet's over, won't you?"

"I don't think so, Craig. Look, we'll talk about it later."

"Nope." He hung onto the back of a chair. "I'm not going to sit down unless you say you'll have a drink with me after the banquet."

"Craig!" Bree glanced around and saw that the people sitting near them were watching. She glowered at Craig and said, "All right, you win. One drink after the banquet."

They found two seats near the platform where the alumni committee had already been seated. That's where Bree was supposed to sit, but Craig had a firm grip on her hand, and afraid of making a scene, she caught Dawn's attention, and indicating Craig, shook her head.

He only picked at the conch chowder. He nibbled a hush puppy but ignored the hearts of palm salad, the resin-baked potatoes and the lobster. He talked amiably with the six other people at the table, drank a lot of wine, and flirted with Bree.

When the key lime pie and coffee were served, Carris took the microphone to introduce the glee club and the cheerleaders. Craig averted his face, then—as though against his will—he turned to watch the women who had once been the cutest girls in the junior and senior class. His gaze lingered on Bobbie Lee.

A look of sadness crossed his face. He bit his lip and turned away. He poured himself another glass of wine.

A short man Bree didn't remember won the award for being the baldest man there. She accepted a bouquet for having come the farthest. Nancy Saunders won for having the most children. Miguel was chosen most eligible bachelor and Jean the most eligible bachelorette.

After the awards had been presented, Carris said, "I know we're all concerned about a lady known as Lola. The latest report has her knocking the hell out of Cuba, but the weather bureau isn't sure where she's headed next. We've decided to put off the dance—"

Boos and catcalls filled the room as Carris held up his hands and said, "Hold on. I said we've decided to put it off, I didn't say we were going to cancel it. Most of you are staying through the weekend anyway, so we've decided to hold the dance on Sunday night. Then if the hurricane hits tomorrow night, we'll all head for the high school or whatever other shelter we're directed to. If it doesn't, I'm sure we can find our way to Sloppy Joe's or whatever watering hole takes our fancy. Sunday night we'll have our final dance right here at the Beachcomber."

As the evening drew to a close, Bree tried to think of an excuse for not having a drink with Craig. All she wanted to do was get away from him and go up to her room to wait for Miguel.

But Craig wasn't going to be easy to get away from. "Let's go outside to the patio bar," he said. When Bree hesitated he took her hand. "You promised," he insisted.

One drink. Twenty minutes, thirty at the most. Bree looked at her watch. "Just let me check with the desk," she said.

She asked for the front desk on a house phone. Miguel hadn't yet returned and there were no messages.

"All right," Bree told Craig. "One fast drink."

He led her to a table at the far end of the patio and ordered two brandies. "This is like old times," he said. "You and me together this way."

"We never were together, Craig. Except for the yearbook we never *had* any old times."

He reached for her hand. "But we should have, Bree. It should have been you all along instead of Bobbie Lee. Did you see her tonight? Did you see the way she's let herself go? She—"

Bree started up from her chair. "I didn't come out here with you to listen to you bad-mouth Bobbie," she said.

"I'm sorry." Craig took her hand and pulled her back down. "I shouldn't have said that. It's just that it kills me to see the way she is now." He tasted the brandy. "Bobbie and I had some good years, Bree. I loved her, maybe I still do. Maybe I'm to blame for the drinking."

Craig looked at Bree. "She lost a baby. That was hard on both of us but it was especially hard on Bobbie. She started drinking right after that. I tried to help her, but I guess I just didn't know what to do. So I did the worst thing I could have, I got involved with somebody else." He picked up the snifter again and his hand was shaking. "I'm not proud of what I did, Bree, but I got to thinking this life is so damn short, that I was running out of time. All of a sudden I wanted everything I could get before it was too late."

"Too late? What in the world are you talking about, Craig? You're thirty-three years old! You've got your whole life ahead of you."

Craig shook his head. "No, I haven't, Bree. It's almost over for me."

Bree thought he was joking, that because he was drunk he was wallowing in self-pity. But she looked at him and saw the fear in his face. "What is it, Craig?" she asked. "Are you ill?"

He rubbed his left shoulder. "Do you remember my father?"

"No, I don't think I do."

"That's because he died when I was eight." Craig looked at her. "He was thirty-three years old when a heart attack killed him, Bree. His father—my grandfather—was thirty-four. It runs in our family, it's in our genes." He signaled for the waiter and ordered two more brandies. "I'm like them, Bree. There's no escaping it. My time's running out. It's—"

"Stop it, Craig." Bree covered his hand with hers. "Have you seen a doctor?"

"A doctor can't help me."

"That's ridiculous and you know it. You're going to make an appointment with a cardiologist on Monday. If you don't I'm going to do it for you."

"No!" His face paled. "I won't go. I know what he'll tell me."

"No, you don't! My God, Craig, just because your father died when he was young—"

"And my grandfather."

"All right, and your grandfather. That doesn't mean the same thing's going to happen you. A lot has happened in medicine in twenty years. If you feel that something's wrong, that maybe you have a heart problem, then for heaven's sake go to a doctor.'' Bree hesitated. ''Have you talked to Bobbie about this?''

Craig shook his head. ''No, I couldn't tell her. I didn't want her to think I was a coward.'' He moved closer to Bree. ''Oh, God, I must be drunk! I've told you and now *you'll* think I'm a coward.''

''Craig...'' Bree took his hand. ''I don't think you're a coward and neither will Bobbie when you tell her. I think you should tell her, Craig. She's your wife.''

''We're separated.''

''But she's still your wife, Craig, and I'll bet anything she still loves you.'' She squeezed his hand. ''You can't go on this way. You're going to see a doctor on Monday if I have to drag you there kicking and screaming.''

Craig took a deep breath. ''Will you go with me?''

Bree nodded. ''Of course I will.''

''Okay.'' He ran a nervous hand through his hair. ''Okay, Bree, I'll go.''

He began to talk then, about his marriage and about the affair he'd had. His voice became slurred. His eyes were red-rimmed and his tie was askew. Craig Logan had been the boy who'd had it all, and it saddened Bree to watch him.

But Craig hadn't had it all, he hadn't had the most important thing...his father. How long, she wondered, had he lived with his fear of dying? Was that why he drank too much? Was that why he'd had the affair?

The hour grew late. Craig talked and talked and talked. And Bree, because he was an old friend and she knew he needed this catharsis, let him continue.

When at last Craig stood up he swayed and clutched the back of his chair. "'Fraid I had a l'il too much to drink, Breezy. Everything's spinning. Don't think I can make it up to my room."

"It's all right, Craig. I'll help you." Bree looked around the patio. The bar had closed and there was no one around. With a smothered sigh she put her arm around his waist. Slowly she walked him across the patio and through the thankfully empty lobby to the elevators.

"L'il Bree," he chortled. "You turned out to be a real beauty. I kissed you once. 'Member? The night of the prom. Don't think I'd ever really seen you till that night. We danced, didn't we?"

"Yes, we danced." She leaned him against the bank of the elevator, trying with all her strength to hold him up.

"An' I kissed you," he said again. "'Member that, Breezy? I kissed you."

"Yes, Craig, I remember." She got him in the elevator and propped him up against one wall. He stumbled and grabbed her shoulder for support. She felt her dress rip and smothered an oath because this was the first time she'd worn it.

When they reached their floor Bree draped one of Craig's arms over her shoulder and started down the hall to his room. At his door she waited while he searched for his key.

When he fumbled for the lock she took it away from him, opened the door and propelled him inside. He staggered to the bed and slumped down. "Think I'm a l'il drunk," he mumbled.

"A little?" Bree said grimly. She took his shoes off, then his jacket. "Try to get some sleep, Craig," she said.

"Not tired." He loosened his tie and reached for her, clasping one hand against the back of her head and disheveling her hair. "Kissed you once," he said. "'Member?"

"Yes, Craig, I remember."

"Okay if I kiss you again?"

"I don't think so, Craig."

He nodded solemnly. "Whatever you say." He unbuttoned his shirt. "Help me out of this, will you, Breezy?"

Bree did as he asked, then straightened and said. "Good night, Craig. I'll see you tomorrow."

"Tomorrow and tomorrow and tomorrow." He struggled to his feet. "I'm a gentleman. Gentlemen walk their ladies to the door."

"You don't have to," Bree said as he clutched her arm. Then with a sigh she opened the door and stepped out into the hall.

"Thank you." Craig bowed from the waist and she put out a hand to steady him. He grinned at her, then suddenly his face sobered. "You're nice, Breezy." His lips brushed hers. He put his arms around her. "I'm drunk and you're my..." He hiccupped. "My good ol' pal," he said just as the elevator doors opened and Miguel stepped out into the hall.

Over Bree's shoulder, Craig said, "Hi, Mike. How're you doing?"

She turned. Miguel stood frozen, staring at her as she disentangled herself from Craig's arms.

"Gotta go to bed," Craig said. "G'night everybody." He grinned a lopsided grin, then staggered in and closed the door.

Bree and Miguel stared at each other. "Miguel," she said. "Miguel, it's not the way it looks. It—"

"My God, Bree," he said, his voice pained. Before Bree could speak again he turned and went down the hall to his room.

Chapter Nine

Miguel stood in the darkness feeling as though he'd received a blow to his heart. The image of Bree in Craig's arms burned past his eyes into his brain and thudded against his skull. He clenched his hands, trying to control his anger—his need to strike out at something, anything—to ease the terrible pain of what he'd seen.

Bree had been with Craig, in Craig's room. Her hair had been disheveled, the shoulder of her dress had been torn. Craig, wearing only his trousers, had looked happily rumpled when he'd kissed her goodnight.

Miguel ran a hand across his face as a low moan escaped his lips. For the second time in his life he'd let Bree make a fool of him. Nothing had changed.

Miguel went out to the balcony. The sound of the waves usually comforted him; tonight it only added to his pain because it brought back old memories of Bree and of the prom night when they'd kissed and knelt together on the sand. And new memories of the past two days they'd spent at sea.

None of it, not one minute of it, had been real. The sighs and whispers, the small cries of passion when she'd lifted her body to his, hadn't meant a thing to her. It was, after all, Craig that she still wanted. Once again, Miguel had been a foil to draw Craig to her.

The phone rang—and continued to ring, unanswered.

Tomorrow morning he'd check out of the hotel. In another week, two at the most, Bree would be on her way back to Paris and he could begin forgetting her.... He closed his eyes. How could he ever forget the sea-green color of her eyes and the way the sun turned her hair to gold, the soft rise of her breasts and the lips that had trembled under his. Or the way she'd whispered his name in the quiet of the night.

Miguel's face tightened with pain. He'd fallen in love with Bree all over again. And, God help him, he'd come this close to asking her to marry him.

Miguel sat out on the balcony until the first faint rays of the sun crept over the sea. Finally, exhausted, he went inside. But his sleep was filled with dreams of Bree and when the painful memory of the night was too great to bear, he got up and dressed and checked out of the hotel.

He turned on the radio in the pickup in time to catch the weather forecast. Hurricane Lola had passed over Cuba, leaving that country devastated. Over two hundred people had died in the storm and homes had been destroyed. Waves twenty feet high were still lashing the *malecon*. The control tower at Havana

Airport had been toppled, forcing the airport to close. Now the storm had stalled somewhere between the Cuban coast and Key West. It was anybody's guess what was going to happen next.

Miguel's main concerns—his only concerns, he told himself—were his home, his family, and the fleet of shrimp boats. As soon as he got to the dock he called Pedro Gonzalez, the man who did odd jobs at the house, and asked him to start boarding up. Then he began his check on the fleet. At eight o'clock Lupita came in to tell him that she and his father had been up since dawn preparing the feast.

"Uncle Manuel dug the pit yesterday," Lupita said. "He'll start roasting the pig this morning. The ingredients for the paella are ready, the *frijoles* are cooking and the beef for the *carne asada* is marinating." She looked out of the window and frowned. "I heard on the weather report that the storm is stalled somewhere out at sea. What time are you going to pick Bree up?"

Miguel stared at her incredulously. The party? My God, she was talking about the party tonight! His brows drew together in a frown and he said, "But we can't have a party. Dad's got to call it off. We've got too much to do here." He shook his head angrily. "This is ridiculous, Lupita! A hurricane's about to hit Key West and you're talking about a party!"

"Dad's determined to have it, Miguel. I don't think you can make him change his mind." Lupita put her hand on his arm. "Maybe it'll all work out. Maybe the storm won't hit after all. If it does we'll just have one big hurricane party."

"But damn it, Lupita, this is dangerous. Dad and I are going to be busy all day trying to make sure the boats will be safe."

"I know, Miguel. But honestly, Uncle Manuel's got everything under control. Aunt Maria and Aunt Consuelo arrived at the house just before I left. Everybody's pitching in. Papa'd be awfully disappointed if we called it off now."

Miguel's face was grim. "Where is he?"

"He dropped me off and went down to the docks." Lupita shook her head. "But I don't think you're going to talk him out of the party, Miguel."

Frowning at her, he went to the chart on the wall to study the red markers that indicated where the boats were. "Any news of the *Lady Ann*?"

"She called in from Shark River an hour ago. Dad told her captain to hole up in Oyster Bay until we know what's going to happen to Lola. She'll be okay there."

The marine radio crackled and Miguel spoke into the microphone. "Alpha bravo yankee. Go ahead."

"This is the *Dipsy Doodle*. That you, Mike?"

"Yeah, Captain Bob." Miguel looked at the chart. What's your location?"

"North side of the Marquesas headed for home."

"What's the weather like?"

"Not too much wind but the sea's picking up. I'll be mighty glad to see Mallory Dock and your smiling face. I got a feeling in my bones that it's gonna be a helluva blow."

"Yeah, so do I," Miguel said. When he'd signed off he went down to the dock and spent the rest of the morning trying not to think about Bree, and arguing with his father about the party.

But Antonio refused to be moved—the party was going on as scheduled, storm or no storm.

At noon, Antonio suggested they break for lunch. "I've gotta check with Manuel," he said. "I want to make sure everything's all right for tonight." He looked up at the sky. "I hope it doesn't rain. We've got thirty-seven people coming. If it rains, the house is going to bust at the seams. You're picking up Bree and her mother, aren't you?"

"I'm going to be busy here, Dad," Miguel hedged. "The *Lady Ann* hasn't come in yet. One of us should stick around the office. It's your party. You have a good time. I'll stay here and monitor the radio."

"Like hell you will. You're my son and this is a family party. Your big reunion dance has been postponed until tomorrow, so you have no excuse. We have a radio at home, we can monitor it there." Antonio looked at him. "Is there something wrong between you and Bree?"

"There was never anything right between us." Miguel started toward the office. Over his shoulder he said, "I'll have Lupita call Bree and explain that I'm tied up because of the storm."

Antonio went after him. Grabbing Miguel's arm, he turned him around. "You make an appearance tonight, Miguel Francisco Alejandro," he said firmly. "You dance with your aunts and your cousins. You eat some food and drink some wine, and you be nice to Bree and her mother because they're our guests. Is that clear?"

Miguel glared at his father. Then he gave an abrupt nod. "I'll be there," he said.

* * *

It was late in the afternoon when Lupita called Bree. "Miguel wanted to pick you and your mother up, but he's tied up here because of the storm. Would you like me to come by for you?"

"No, thanks, Lupita, I still have the rental car." Bree hesitated. "I thought you might cancel the party—because of the storm, I mean."

Lupita laughed. "When Papa says he's going to have a party, he's going to have a party. We've got dozens of relatives all set for a feast, Bree, there's no backing out now. Besides, the hurricane is still stalled out at sea trying to make up its mind what it's going to do." Another phone rang and Lupita said, "I've got to go, Bree. We'll see you about six."

Bree frowned as she put the phone down. She didn't want to go to the party, not after what had happened last night, but she didn't know any way to get out of it. She'd talked to her mother this morning, and although Cornelia had sputtered that she really didn't want to go to "that man's house," she'd told Bree that she'd decided to wear her blue dress and that she was getting her hair done at noon.

"I wish you'd spend the night with me," Cornelia had said. "Just in case the storm does hit I'd feel better if you were here with me. If it sputters out you can go on back to the hotel in the morning."

Bree had agreed. She'd already decided that she and her mother wouldn't stay long at the party. She wouldn't be going in the first place if she hadn't already promised Antonio.

Bree winced as she thought of last night. As long as she lived she'd never forget the look on Miguel's face when he stepped off the elevator.

She'd started down the hall after him, then decided it might be better to wait a few minutes to let him cool off. When she went in her room and switched on the light she'd caught a look at herself in the mirror. Her hair had been a mess. Her lipstick was smeared and one shoulder of her dress had been ripped. She'd grasped the edge of the dresser and smothered a moan. No wonder Miguel had been upset!

Bree tried to call him to explain that what he'd seen wasn't what he thought it was, but he hadn't answered the phone. She'd tried again this morning, only to be told that Mr. Rivas had checked out of the hotel very early. She'd paced her room, then called him at the office. He was down on the docks, Lupita told her, but she'd give him the message and he'd call as soon as he came in.

But Miguel didn't call. The only word she'd had was when Lupita called to say that he'd be tied up at the dock all day.

Don't panic, Bree told herself, you'll see him tonight. But she knew that a party was the worst place to try to have a serious conversation.

Bree spent a miserable afternoon in her room. Finally, because she couldn't stand being alone any longer, she got in the car and drove to her mother's.

When Cornelia opened the door, Bree gasped. She couldn't remember ever seeing her mother's hair in anything but the slicked-back topknot she always wore. But now her mother's naturally wavy hair was swept up into a softly flattering chignon.

"You look beautiful!" Bree said.

Cornelia blushed. "I'm just trying to make a decent impression—for you. You seem so fond of the Rivas family that I'm willing to put aside my feelings for the night." She patted her hair. "Do I really look all right?"

Bree hugged her mother. "You look wonderful."

"What time are we supposed to be there?"

"Six." Bree looked at her watch. "We've got plenty of time."

"I'm sorry your dance had to be postponed but I'm sure you're just as pleased to be going to the Rivas party, seeing how well you and Miguel are getting along. Is he going to pick us up?"

"No, he isn't. He's . . . busy because of the storm. I imagine he'll come later."

"Is everything all right?"

"Yes, of course." Bree avoided her mother's gaze. "I think I'll go up to my room and try to find something to wear."

"Why don't you wear that pretty white dress? The ruffly off-the-shoulder one."

Bree nodded. "All right," she said listlessly.

Cornelia looked at her, then after a moment's hesitation said, "You look tired, Bree. Why don't you rest for a little while?"

"Yes, I think I will." Bree kissed her mother's cheek. "Call me at five, will you?"

"Yes, dear." A frown of concern puckered Cornelia's brow as she watched Bree go up the stairs.

They could hear the beat of the Latin music when they parked the car. Bree glanced at her mother in time to see Cornelia's lips tighten. "We won't stay long," Bree said.

Over and above the music they could hear the laughter and talk that was part Cuban Spanish and part English. Whole passels of children shrieked and giggled and ran through the house and into the yard. The smell of roast pig permeated the air.

Cornelia took a deep breath as they went up the walk. "My word," she whispered as she shook her head as though trying to clear it. "Do we really have to—"

The door burst open and Antonio said, "*Bienvenidas*, welcome to our house. Come in, come in. You look beautiful. Like sisters." He took Cornelia's arm and led her inside. "Let me introduce you and Bree to everybody," he said. "Miguel isn't here yet, but he's coming. Ah, here are Aunt Sophia and Uncle Carlos."

There followed an introduction of aunts and uncles and cousins in confusing numbers. Bree's head was swimming and Cornelia looked stunned when one of the cousins thrust a baby into her arms and said, "This is little Juanito. He's two months old today."

Cornelia cleared her throat. "What a lovely child," she managed to say as she looked down at the baby who looked up at her and began to howl. "I . . . I'm afraid he wants his mother," she said.

"Si, si." Antonio grinned as he took the baby from Cornelia and handed it back to his mother. "How can Señora Petersen hold your baby and a glass of rum punch at the same time?" He picked two tall glasses off a tray and said, "Here you are, ladies. *Salud!*" Then, before Cornelia could object, he said, "Excuse us, Bree. Your mother and I are going to dance."

Cornelia shot one shocked, alarmed look at Bree as Antonio took her hand and led her toward the music coming from the back yard—leaving Bree with the aunts and uncles and cousins.

Two hours later, just as Lupita called everybody out to the patio for dinner, Miguel arrived. He greeted his relatives, nodded briefly to Bree, then linking his arm with a lovely dark-haired young woman Lupita's age, he followed the others out to the patio where Lupita and several of the aunts were placing heaping platters of food on the tables. He seated the young woman, then went to the other tables to speak to everyone.

When he came to where Bree and her mother were sitting he said, "Good evening, Mrs. Petersen. I'm so glad you could come." His gaze rested on Bree for a moment. "I hope you're having a good time," he said politely. "I'm sorry I wasn't able to pick you up."

"That's quite all right. It's...it's a lovely party," Bree said.

Miguel nodded and when he moved on Cornelia said, "Something's happened between the two of you, hasn't it?"

"Yes, Mother. But I don't think I want to talk about it now."

"Very well." Cornelia's voice softened. "But when you do please remember that I'm here."

Halfway through dinner people began to dance to the music of the stereo. Bree had tried to avoid looking at Miguel but it was difficult when he began dancing with the young brunette.

He looked as Latin as the music tonight, dressed in dark pants and a white *guayabera* shirt, gracefully moving to the insistent rhythm. His hair glistened like a crow's wing under the gaily colored lights festooning the patio. Once he glanced Bree's way and their eyes met before he quickly looked away.

Antonio claimed Cornelia for another dance, then continued to dance with her. When Cornelia finally came back to the table she said, "I've never danced so much in my life." She filled her glass with rum punch and took a long drink. "That man is tireless," she said.

Bree forced a smile. "You seemed to be having a good time." She looked at her watch. "It's after eleven..."

But Cornelia wasn't listening, she was looking at Antonio, who'd stopped to speak to Miguel, and there was an expression on her face that Bree had never seen before.

Antonio was angry. "Have you no manners?" he hissed to his son. "Bree is our guest and you're ignoring her. How dare you act this way? I won't have it, Miguel. You go over there now and ask Bree to dance."

"Father..." Miguel took a deep breath. "Very well." He turned on his heel and approached Bree. "Would you like to dance?"

Bree looked up at him, then wet her lips. "Yes, I...yes, thank you."

Miguel took her hand and led her out to the patio. The white ruffled dress floated around her ankles, and her golden hair brushed her shoulders. He could smell her perfume and the faint aroma of the pink camellia tucked behind one ear.

"Miguel..." Bree cleared her throat. "We have to talk. I have to explain, to tell you what happened last night."

"There's no need to explain, Bree. Everything's quite clear."

"No, it isn't! You don't understand about Craig. He desperately needed somebody to talk to last night." Her fingers tightened around Miguel's hand. "He got drunk Miguel, and I tried to help him. I took him to his room and—"

"Undressed him?" he snapped.

"I helped him off with his jacket, that's all." She looked up at him. "I know the way it looked when you saw us together in the hall, Miguel, but that's not the way it was."

"Isn't it funny how things never really change?" he said coldly. "You think they do, you pray that they will—you even dream that some day everything will be just the way you want it to be. But nothing ever really changes, Bree. Neither do people."

Miguel took a deep breath and stepping away from her said, "You'll have to excuse me. I checked with the weather bureau a few minutes ago. The storm has started to move again. I have to get back to the office."

"Miguel, please."

He shook his head. "We've said all there is to say, Bree." He took her arm and led her back to her table and when she was seated he said to Cornelia, "I'm afraid I have to leave now, Mrs. Petersen. I hope you'll stay as long as you like and enjoy the party." He glanced at Bree before he turned and walked away.

"Would you like to leave?" Cornelia asked quietly.

"Yes, Mother, if you don't mind."

"Of course I don't mind. But we must find Lupita and Antonio and thank them." She stood up and when she did Antonio rushed over.

"You're not leaving?" he said. "The party's just beginning."

"I'm sorry." Bree squeezed the bridge of her nose. "I have a headache, Antonio. I really think I need to rest."

"Ay, *muchacha*." He put his arm around her shoulder and with a fatherly hug said, "I'm sorry. Would you like me to drive you home?"

"No, thanks. I have the car." She took her mother's arm. "It's a lovely party and we've enjoyed it. Thank you for inviting us."

"Yes, thank you." Cornelia offered her hand. "It's been very nice. Really."

"But you're not going, Cornelia. I won't hear of it. If Bree must go I'll understand, but you..." He shook his head. "No, that's impossible!" He turned to Bree. "I'll take your mother home whenever she's ready," he said. "She'll dance some more and drink some more. Then I'll take her home."

Bree looked at her mother. "Yes, by all means stay if you want to."

"Of course she wants to." Antonio put his arm around Cornelia and gave her a squeeze.

Bree waited for her mother's back to stiffen and for her to step away.

But Cornelia stayed where she was. She looked up at Antonio and with a blush turned to Bree. "If you don't mind going home alone, dear..."

Bree stared at her mother in surprise. "No," she said quickly. "No, of course I don't mind." She kissed her mother's cheek. "I'll go find Lupita now. Thanks again for a wonderful party, Antonio."

When Bree got into the car, she sat for a moment. She felt more tired than she'd ever felt in her life and she wished that she'd never left Paris. She didn't want to smell the night-blooming jasmine or listen to the cry of the katydids. The soft warm southern air against her skin seemed to stir too many memories. She had to talk to Miguel. She had to make him understand.

Bree started the car and headed down to Mallory Docks, but she hesitated once she got there. Miguel was angry, he'd resent her coming, but she had to talk to him. Taking a deep breath, she locked the car door, then went up the stairs leading to his office.

Bree heard the static sound of the marine radio, and another radio playing a fast, modern beat. She knocked tentatively, and when there was no answer, she opened the door.

Miguel stood in front of the marine radio. The pretty dark-haired girl from the party stood behind him. She was barefoot, her arms were around Miguel's waist as she pressed her body to his while she did in-place dance steps. Suddenly she looked around and saw Bree. An uncertain smile crossed her face. "Well, hi."

"Hi."

The word hung in the air as Miguel swung around.

"I'm sorry," Bree whispered, "I didn't know—I thought you'd be working. Oh, God, I'm sorry."

Before either Miguel or the young woman could speak, Bree ran out the door and down the stairs. She heard Miguel call out to her but didn't stop. She fled to her car, searching in her purse for the keys as she ran.

As she wheeled the car around, she looked up and saw Miguel standing in the doorway of his office. She looked away, and blinded by tears, sped away from the docks.

It was late. Bree sat up in bed, listening to a Jimmy Buffett tape because Jimmy Buffett *was* Key West. She'd taken tapes of his songs to Paris with her to play on cold winter nights when the wind blew down the Champs Élysées and she felt very far from home. Now as he began to sing she scrunched down in bed and hugging a pillow, let the tears fall unheeded. She cried for a long time, until finally exhausted, she fell into a restless sleep. When she awoke she got up and went into the bathroom to splash cold water on her face.

Back in the bedroom again she glanced at the clock. It was almost three-fifteen. She opened her bedroom door and went to the top of the stairs. The light was still on in the living room; which meant her mother was still at the party!

Her own worries forgotten now, Bree paced her bedroom. At four o'clock she put on her robe and went downstairs to make a pot of coffee. Every five minutes she pulled back an edge of the living-room curtain and peered out into the darkness. Once she went to the phone, meaning to dial the Rivas house, then put it down and told herself she'd wait another fifteen minutes.

At four-thirty she heard a car stop in front of the house and a wave of relief flooded through her, to be replaced almost immediately by blazing anger. Where had her mother been? What had she been thinking of to come rolling in at this time of night? This *morning*? It was almost daylight!

When she heard steps approaching, Bree backed up to the stairs. She waited. And waited. Fifteen minutes went by before she heard Cornelia's key in the lock and a whispered, "Good night."

The door opened and closed. Cornelia stepped into the room.

"Well!" Bree approached, hands on her hips, chin thrust forward. "Do you have any idea what time it is?" she demanded. "Where in the world have you . . . ?'' She stopped and stared at her mother, too surprised to speak.

Cornelia's face was flushed. Her hair had loosened from the chignon and fell softly about her face. She was in stocking feet, her shoes in one hand.

Bree looked at her, too surprised to speak. "My feet were tired," Cornelia said with a sigh. "We danced and danced . . . it was a wonderful night, Bree." She hiccuped gently. "The best night of my life."

"You're . . . you're *tipsy*!" Bree sputtered. "And you've been..." She couldn't keep the indignation out of her voice. "You've been making out!"

"Yes, dear." Cornelia patted Bree's cheek. Then with a sweet, slow smile she went up the stairs to her room.

Chapter Ten

Bree awoke the next morning to the smell of bacon frying in the kitchen and Cornelia's voice raised in song. When the words to "Oh, What a Beautiful Morning" floated up to her, Bree remembered last night, or rather this morning when her mother had finally come in. She looked at the clock and saw that it was almost noon and shook her head in bewilderment. Her mother, no matter what time she'd gone to bed, always got up at seven o'clock sharp.

Cornelia didn't have a frivolous bone in her body. She'd always been straitlaced and as prim as a starched napkin. When her mother had visited her in Paris, five years after Bree's father's death, Bree had suggested it was time, given the opportunity, that her mother begin dating. Cornelia had drawn herself up to her full five foot three inches and glared at Bree, demanding how she could have even suggested such a thing.

Last night Cornelia had danced with Antonio Rivas, a man she'd professed to dislike for the past ten or so years. She'd let him bring her home and she'd obviously let him kiss her good-night. A slow smile crossed Bree's face, to be quickly replaced by a look of bitterness. What was it about the Rivas men that made the Petersen women find them so attractive?

Miguel was the most attractive man she'd ever known. Bree wasn't sure how it had happened but somehow, in the past few days, she'd fallen in love with him. She didn't know whether or not he was in love with her but she knew there was something between them—or at least there had been.

Making love with Miguel had been unlike anything Bree had ever known before, but what they'd shared had been much, much more than making love. She'd felt *loved*. In his arms she'd known a sense of coming home, of belonging. It was as though she'd found the other half of herself, the half that at last made her complete—which, despite her singlemindedness, was something her career had never done.

Miguel's embrace had warmed and comforted her. Even when his masculinity had been overwhelming, when he moved so fiercely and forcefully against her, she'd somehow known he would never take her beyond what she could bear. When at last she'd broken free to soar with him to the heights of passion, he'd held her so close she could feel the beating of his heart. He'd whispered her name against her throat and told her that he'd never before experienced the joy she'd given him.

He'd soothed her and held her cradled in his arms and she'd thought she would die with loving him.

It had been so right, so infinitely right between them. But now . . . ? Tears flooded Bree's eyes and she sat up in bed and reached for a tissue. She didn't blame Miguel for being angry, because she knew how it must have looked to him when he stepped off the elevator. If she'd been in his place—but she *had* been in Miguel's place last night. He'd taken that young woman to the office with him when he left the party. Had he taken her home with him later? Bree pressed the tips of her fingers against her eyes as though trying to blot out the picture of Miguel and the lovely brunette.

She wished that she'd never come home to Key West, that she'd never seen Miguel again. She wanted to erase the memory of that night on the boat.

"Bree?" Her mother's voice, sounding strangely light and musical, floated up the stairs. "Breakfast is ready."

Taking a deep breath and trying to sound cheerful, Bree called out, "I'll be right down."

She went into the bathroom and bathed her eyes so that her mother wouldn't know she'd been crying. When she came out of the bathroom Cornelia was singing again. Bree paused and a small frown puckered her brow. Something very strange had happened to her mother and she was going to find out what it was. Quickly she pulled on her robe and went downstairs.

"Good morning," she said when she went into the kitchen, but she stopped and stared when she saw her mother. Cornelia's hair had been pulled back into a ponytail and tied with a blue ribbon. What in the world was happening to her?

The doorbell rang before Bree could ask that question.

"I'll get it," Cornelia said. Bree heard the murmur of voices, then her mother returned to the kitchen, carrying a long white florist's box.

"Flowers," Cornelia said. "I bet they're from Miguel." She raised the lid. "Red roses! Aren't they lovely?" She handed Bree the box.

Thank God, Bree thought. It was going to be all right. He would explain about last night—and he would let her tell him what really happened with Craig. With shaking fingers she opened the small white envelope tucked among the red roses and looked at the card.

It read, "Thank you for an unforgettable evening. I'll pick you up tonight at eight." It was signed Antonio.

Bree swallowed. "They're for you," she said.

"For me?" Cornelia blushed. She read the proffered card and her faced turned even pinker. "That man," she said, looking pleased. She lifted the two dozen red roses out of the box and held them against her face.

Bree tried to swallow her disappointment. "Would you like me to put them in water for you?" she asked.

Cornelia nodded. "The milk-glass vase is on the top shelf. I think that would look nice, don't you?" She looked at Bree and suddenly realized her daughter's unhappiness. "Oh, darling, I'm sorry. You thought they were from Miguel, didn't you?"

"Yes, I suppose I did." Bree turned away, and standing on her tiptoes managed to reach the vase. When she put it on the table, she tried to turn the conversation away from herself. "You know that I'm dying of curiosity, don't you? You've always called Antonio 'that man,' but the words sounded different when you said them just now." She smiled at her mother. "I take it you had a good time last night?"

"I had a wonderful time, Bree. I didn't expect... well, you know I didn't really want to go to the party. When we arrived I was appalled that there were so many people, all that noise and confusion, the loud music. But after a while... I don't know, I suppose I got used to it." She began putting the roses in the vase. "Antonio is a wonderful dancer." Cornelia sighed. "Just wonderful."

"What time did the party break up?"

"A little after two."

"But you didn't come in until four-thirty." Bree folded her arms across her chest. "Why were you so late?"

"Well, I... I helped Antonio and Lupita clean up. Then we listened to some music and we talked and I suppose I forgot about the time. I hope you weren't worried."

"Of course I was worried," Bree said sternly. "I thought something might have happened to you. You should have called. You should have..." Then, as though realizing the absurdity of the situation, she laughed and said, "I'm glad you had a good time, mother. Are you going to see Antonio tonight?"

"Yes, if the hurricane doesn't blow us all right into the ocean. He's terribly worried about the shrimp boats. If the storm hits he and Miguel will be out in the thick of it." Cornelia's eyes softened with concern. "Why don't you tell me what's happened between you and Miguel, dear?"

Bree sighed and went to the stove and poured herself a cup of coffee. When she sat down she said, "Miguel didn't go to the banquet the night before last. He had to monitor the incoming boats because of the storm, but he told me he'd get back to the hotel later that night."

"Didn't he come back?"

"Yes, he did, but..." Bree told her mother how the evening progressed and about Craig's brotherly kiss. "Miguel saw us," Bree said. "He saw Craig with his arms around me, kissing me."

"But didn't you explain?"

"I tried to but Miguel disappeared so fast I didn't have a chance. I called him but he wouldn't answer the phone and the next morning he checked out of the hotel. Then last night when we danced I tried to tell what had happened but he didn't want to talk about it. He was so...so cold, mother. His face was so closed."

Bree put her hands around the coffee cup as though trying to warm them. "I went down to his office after the party. I thought if we were alone I could explain about Craig." She looked across the table at her mother. "But he wasn't alone."

"Oh. Oh, dear." Cornelia covered Bree's hand with her own. Without a word she got up and dished bacon, scrambled eggs and grits onto their plates. When she sat down she said, "You care a great deal about him, don't you?"

"Yes." Bree's throat tightened. "I do and I thought he cared about me as well. But he didn't, Mother. I was just a...a fling for old time's sake." Her voice hardened. "Let's give the little lady from Paris a whirl while she's here so she'll have something to remember us by."

"Stop it!" Cornelia set her coffee cup down with such force that the coffee spilled over onto the saucer. "Don't you dare belittle yourself or whatever it is that has passed between you and Miguel. Miguel's a decent man. He's upset, and rightfully so, over what he thinks happened between you and Craig." She sniffed. "That Craig Logan, feeling sorry for himself and compromising you. He should be talking to Bobbie Lee instead of you. *She's* his wife."

Cornelia buttered a hot biscuit and handed it to Bree. "I know that poor girl has let herself go and that she drinks too much, but maybe she wouldn't if Craig hadn't found himself a young somebody down at Plantation." Cornelia bit into a piece of bacon and added rather fiercely, "I'd like to thump him good for causing trouble between you and Miguel."

"I thought you didn't like Miguel—that you've never liked him."

"I liked him well enough," Cornelia said defensively. "I thought he had a lot of courage, working down on the docks while he was going to high school, and not being able to take part in any of the school activities like the rest of you."

"But you didn't approve of my tutoring him."

"Of course I didn't, dear. I saw the way he was looking at you back then—like you were the whipped cream on top of a piece of key lime pie. He could never keep his eyes off you. It scared the living daylights out of me because I thought you felt the same way about him and that things might get out of hand."

"But I didn't like him then—not that way, I mean."

"But I didn't know that. You were such a quiet mouse of a girl, never telling anybody how you felt. I can imagine your being so crazy about Craig must have hurt Miguel deeply."

Cornelia shook her head at Bree. "Young girls are foolish as peahens," she snapped. "I remember the night of the prom. Miguel was all slicked up, looking as handsome as could be. Your father tried to make conversation but poor Miguel was so nervous he couldn't say two words. Then your father announced you and Miguel stood up and saw you coming down the stairs."

Cornelia took a deep, shaking breath. "I thought I'd cry right there on the spot because you looked so beautiful, Bree. Then I looked at Miguel. I saw the expression on his face and my heart almost stopped because I knew he was seeing you just the way I was, and that he loved you almost as much."

Bree stared at her mother. "I...I never knew," she whispered. "I never knew he felt that way." She lowered her head. I didn't know you felt that way either, she thought.

Later, in her own room, Bree sat before the old-fashioned vanity that had been a present for her sixteenth birthday. She looked at the pictures that were still tucked around the mirror. There was one of her and Dawn at the beach when they were fifteen—she smiled because Dawn's figure showed all the swelling promise of womanhood, while her own looked all gangling arms and legs. Above the picture was one of Jean, Eleanor, Frannie, Dawn and herself. And above that there was a picture of Craig. There were no pictures of Miguel.

Had her mother been right? Had Miguel liked her, in that special boy-girl way, fifteen years ago? Was that why he'd been so furious the night of the prom? Because he'd seen Craig kissing her? Bree stared at herself in the mirror. Just as he'd seen Craig kissing her two nights ago. It must have seemed to Miguel that it was prom night all over again—that history was repeating itself. Had he, after all these years, kept the memory of that night?

She made up her mind; she would see Miguel today and she'd make him listen, and she wouldn't think about the young woman she'd seen him with at the office.

But when Bree called Miguel's office Lupita told her that he was out on the dock working with the shrimp-boat captains who were rafting the boats, aligning them in what seemed like a more sheltered part of the dock.

"We keep checking with the weather bureau," Lupita said. "But they're still not sure what the storm is doing or where it's going. They've been flying reconnaissance planes out all morning. Apparently the storm is just hovering and gaining strength. At this point it's anybody's guess what's going to happen." The marine radio crackled and Lupita said, "Hang on a minute, Bree."

Bree heard Lupita's voice and the crackling voice on the other end of the radio. When Lupita came back on the line she said, "That was the *Lady Ann*." Lupita sounded worried. "She's been anchored up at Oyster Bay but her skipper says he's heading for home. I tried to argue him out of it but he wouldn't listen to me. I know he should stay where he is until we know whether the storm's coming our way or not. Look,

Bree, I'd better run on down to the docks and tell Dad and Miguel.'' She hesitated. ''Is the dance tonight being called off?''

''No, they're going ahead with it. The committee decided if the storm hits and the lights go off we can always dance by candlelight.''

''I don't think that's wise.'' Bree could hear the concern in Lupita's voice. ''The Beachcomber isn't that far from the ocean. If we get the storm there'll be some big waves coming in. Everybody should get as far from the water as they can. You really ought to talk Dawn and the others into calling off the dance, Bree.''

''I'm going over to the hotel in a little while, Lupita. I'll talk to her.''

''I've got to run now, Bree. Listen, I...'' Lupita cleared her throat. ''I know this isn't any of my business, but have you and Miguel had a misunderstanding?''

''Yes, I guess we have.''

''I thought so.'' Lupita's sigh was audible. ''He's been a bear the last two days.'' The radio crackled again. ''If there's anything I can do...''

''I know, Lupita. Thanks.''

The phone clicked.

An hour later Bree kissed her mother goodbye. ''I'll call you later,'' she said. ''If the storm does veer this way, I'll come right home. We'll sit it out together, either here or at a shelter.''

Bree drove the car toward the hotel, but halfway there she saw a phone booth and pulled over. Flipping through the pages she found Craig and Bobbie's names listed. Getting back in the car she headed for the address.

It was a nice white house on a quiet street. But the grass hadn't been mowed in weeks and the house itself had a run-down, almost deserted look. Bree stopped in front, hesitated, then got out of the car and headed up the walk. The front door was open, and the screen door hung by one hinge.

"Hello," she called. "Anybody home?"

"Who is it? Hang on a minute, I'm coming." Bobbie Lee, her hair disheveled, wearing faded shorts and a man's shirt that hung low over her hips, padded barefoot to the door.

"Hi," she said when she saw Bree. "This is a...a surprise. Uh, come in."

"Hi, Bobbie. I hope I'm not bothering you."

"No, I...no of course not. Sit down, please. Would you like a cup of coffee or a drink or something?"

"No, thanks." Bree followed Bobbie into a living room that was strewn with newspapers and magazines and smelled of stale cigarette smoke. A half-empty can of beer sat on the cluttered coffee table.

"Gee, I'm sorry." Bobbie made a halfhearted attempt to clear away the papers and magazines. "I wasn't expecting anybody."

"That's okay, don't worry about it. I should have called first but I was on my way back to the hotel when I suddenly thought of you. We haven't really had a chance to visit since I've been here, Bobbie. There've been so many people around all the time. I just suddenly decided I'd run by for a minute and see you."

"I'm really glad you did, Bree." Bobbie reached for a cigarette. "How does it feel to be home?"

"Good, but a little strange. I've enjoyed seeing everybody."

"You've been away for a long time, haven't you? Ever since graduation."

"I came back when my dad died."

"But not since then?"

"No."

"I bet you've seen a lot of changes." Bobbie coughed and smashed the cigarette out in an already too-full ashtray. "A lot of couples who got married right out of high school have split, just like Craig and me."

Bree nodded. "I'm awfully sorry about that, Bobbie."

"Yeah, so am I." Her blue eyes filled with tears. "I miss him so much, Bree."

"Have you tried to talk to him? I mean since the breakup."

Bobbie shook her head. "He came by once, a couple of weeks ago, but I wasn't...I wasn't feeling too well and he left. I guess by now there's somebody else." She looked at Bree. "I wouldn't blame him if there was because I'm such a mess. I'm overweight and my hair looks like the hurricane has already hit. It used to be light blond, Bree, remember? Now it's just this dishwater color."

"It can still be light blond, Bobbie," Bree said with a smile. "And you can knock the weight off." She hesitated, wanting to help Bobbie but afraid to overstep. "You're going to the dance tonight, aren't you?" she asked.

Bobbie shook her head. "I haven't got anything to wear."

"Then let's go shopping and get you something." Bobbie looked surprised but before she could say anything, Bree said, "I've got the rest of the day with nothing to do. I'd love to go shopping with you. And let's both splurge and get our hair done, okay?''

''But I...'' Bobbie took a deep breath. ''I can't go to the party, Bree. I wouldn't have anybody to dance with and Craig will probably be there with somebody else. I'd feel out of place. I know you're trying to be nice, but I just can't face Craig again.''

''Bobbie...'' Bree rested her hand on the other woman's arm. ''I know this is none of my business, Bobbie, but I have a feeling that Craig needs you.''

''Craig needs me?'' Bobbie laughed, a sad little sound that fragmented into tiny fragile pieces. She shook her head. ''No, Bree,'' she managed to say, ''Craig doesn't need me, he's never needed me.''

''I think you're wrong.'' Bree hesitated, wondering whether or not to tell Bobbie about Craig's fears for his health. He'd spoken to her in confidence because they were old friends and because he'd been drunk. She didn't want to betray his confidence and yet...

''I think you're wrong,'' Bree said at last. ''Craig needs you now more than he ever has before.''

When Bobbie looked at her in surprise, Bree took a deep breath and said, ''Craig thinks he's ill, Bobbie. He thinks he's dying.''

Bree told Bobbie Lee everything that Craig had told her the other night. Bobbie shook her head in disbelief. ''I can't believe it, Bree. Craig's always been a little unsure of himself, but I can't believe he really thinks he's dying. If he's so afraid why doesn't he go to a doctor?''

''Because he's afraid of what the doctor might tell him.''

''But that's silly.''

"Of course it's silly. But we're all afraid of things, Bobbie. Most of the time we're scared to death to tell anybody about our fears or ask for help." Bree reached for Bobbie's hand. "I have a feeling you're the only one who can help Craig."

For a long moment Bobbie stared at Bree. "I can try," she said. "We used to be able to tell each other things. Maybe we still can."

"Then you'll go to the dance tonight?"

"I can't, Bree, I don't have a date."

"Neither do I," Bree said as she stood up and headed for the phone. "So we'll go together. Does Donna Marie still own the Clip Joint?"

"Yes, but..."

"No buts, Bobbie. Go make yourself presentable while I make appointments for us."

Twenty minutes later the two women left Bobbie's house and headed down Truman Avenue. While Bree's hair was shampooed and blow-dried, Bobbie's was shampooed, cut, lightened and set. They both had manicures and by the time they left the shop Bobbie looked as pleased as she did surprised.

Their next stop was a new boutique that Bree had spotted on Duval Street. When Bobbie said that she couldn't afford a new dress, Bree insisted it was her treat and refused to listen to Bobbie's protests. Bobbie tried on several things and finally, at Bree's gentle suggestion, settled on a simple but elegant black dress.

"I've got good black pumps," Bobbie said. "They'll go great with the dress."

"Then let's stop by the house and pick them up." When Bobbie stared at her in surprise, Bree said, "I'm feeling blue, Bobbie. I'd really like it if you'd come back to the Beachcomber with me. We could send down for dinner and then dress for the dance. It'll be fun having somebody to talk to while we get ready."

It *was* fun. They sent down for shrimp salads and when Bobbie thought beers would go nicely, Bree suggested having sodas instead.

When it was time to dress Bree helped Bobbie with her makeup. "I got pretty good at this when I was modeling," she said as she touched and softened a bit of pale blue shadow to Bobbie's eyes. Finally she stepped back to examine her handiwork, and truthfully said, "You look absolutely beautiful."

Bobbie's cheeks flushed with pleasure. She turned from the mirror to hug Bree. "You're a good friend," she whispered. "Thank you."

It was while Bree was dressing that they heard the television news flash that Hurricane Lola had suddenly turned and with renewed and even stronger winds was headed right for Key West.

"You are advised to take every precaution," the newsman said. "It's too late to attempt to reach Miami so we're going to announce public shelters you can go to if you live anywhere near the beach. For those folks down in Marathon you're advised to go to either the Marathon Elementary School or Saint Pedro's Catholic Church."

A sudden crash of thunder interrupted his words and lightning flashed across the room.

"This is a violent storm," the newsman continued, "with extremely high winds and gusts reported to be between one hundred and forty and one hundred and fifty miles an hour."

Bree and Bobbie looked at each other. "I'd better finish dressing," Bree said nervously. "You keep listening."

Bree hurried into the bathroom, quickly finished her makeup and hair, and slipped into the dress she'd brought from Paris, a fluid sheath of emerald satin embroidered with sequins. She fastened on emerald earrings and stepped into silver sandals.

When she came out of the bathroom the newscaster was giving the list of shelters. He finished the newscast by saying, "This is a vicious storm, folks, and unless a miracle happens it's going to hit Key West head-on somewhere before midnight. Take every precaution. Get to a shelter and—"

The telephone rang. Bree answered and her mother asked if she'd heard the news.

"Yes, we've got the television on now."

"We?"

"Bobbie Lee is with me, mother."

"Oh? That's nice, Bree. What are you going to do about the dance?"

"I'm not sure. We're going down to the ballroom now to see what's happening. As soon as I check it out I'll come home."

"That's one reason I was calling you, Bree. Antonio is here and he insists that you and I go home with him. He's taking me there now, then he's going down to the dock to check on the boats. He wants you to meet me at his home, Bree. Can you drive over there alone?"

"Yes, of course I can, Mother. But I've got to go downstairs first." The lights flickered and Bree said, "Hang on a minute." To Bobbie she said, "There's a flashlight on the right-hand side of the dresser. You'd better get it."

"I heard you," Cornelia said. "The lights are going off here, too. I've got to go, dear, because Antonio has to get down to the docks. Please come over as soon as you can." Cornelia hesitated. "Antonio wants to talk to you," she said.

His voice boomed strong over the wire. "I don't want you to worry about your mother," he told Bree. "It's a sturdy house. Lupita will be there along with some of the uncles and aunts and I'll get back just as soon as I can. We'll be waiting for you there, Bree, so don't delay too long or your mother will worry."

"I won't, Antonio. And thank you for taking care of Mother." She hesitated, then asked, "What about Miguel? Where is he?"

"Still at the office. He's been on marine radio almost all afternoon trying to raise the *Lady Ann*. There hasn't been any word from Ernie Young, her skipper, since he left Oyster Bay. We told him to stay where he was but he wanted to get back to his family. Your mother and I are going by now to see Ernie's wife. As soon as I get Nellie back to my place I'll go on down to the dock."

Nellie? A smile tugged at the corners of Bree's mouth. He'd called her mother Nellie!

"Miguel says he's going to stay down there on the docks during the storm," Antonio said, "but if Lola's half as wild as they're saying she is I want him to get the hell out of there." She heard his exasperated sigh. "Miguel's got a mind of his own though, and he's as stubborn as a mule when he wants to be. But don't you worry about him, he'll be all right."

Bree put the phone down, her forehead puckered with concern for Miguel. But she didn't speak of her concern when she turned to Bobbie and said, "That's a relief. Mother's going to the Rivas house with Antonio. You and I had better go downstairs and see what's happening.''

The lights flickered again, wavered for a moment, then went out.

Bobbie snapped the flashlight on. "I guess this means we'll take the stairs," she said nervously.

"I guess it does." Bree picked up her evening bag and linking her arm through Bobbie's. "I'm awfully glad you're with me," she said—and meant it.

She was relieved to know that her mother was safe with Antonio, but she didn't like the idea that Miguel would be down on the dock during a hurricane, especially a hurricane with the terrible strength of this one. She wasn't sure the docks were safe.

She wasn't sure that the Beachcomber was safe either.

Chapter Eleven

From the moment Bree and Bobbie stepped into the ballroom it seemed as though they had stepped back in time. Candles glowed from wall sconces and the music coming from the bandstand was soft, reminiscent of a time before electronic devices had taken over the music world. The strains of the 1972 hits floated softly over the room where couples danced.

Dawn, standing near the bar with John, called them over. "Hi, you two," she said. "What do you think of the hurricane news?"

"I'm not sure." Bree looked around the room. "I'm surprised to see so many people here."

"Yes, so am I." Dawn looked curiously at Bree. "Where've you been? I tried to call you this afternoon to tell you we were having an emergency meeting."

"I'm sorry, I was out with Bobbie."

"No harm done. We really didn't decide anything anyway because we weren't sure what was happening with the storm until just a little while ago. We—" Dawn paused and really looked at Bobbie Lee. "You look wonderful, Bobbie," she said.

"Thank you." Bobbie looked embarrassed. "Bree helped me pick out this dress."

"It's lovely and so are you," John said. He looked at Bree. "If the way you're dressed is any indication of how the women look in Paris I'm buying a one-way ticket tomorrow. You look incredible. Wait until Miguel sees you in that dress. Where is he? Held up by the storm?"

"I suppose so," Bree hedged. "What's everybody going to do? Shouldn't there be an announcement about going to the shelters?"

"The storm isn't supposed to hit for hours yet," Dawn told her. "Everybody's here and having such a good time that I don't think they'd leave, storm or no storm. Our best bet is to have the party break up early, in time for all the guests to either go to a shelter or back to their rooms for a hurricane party."

"The weather advisory said people should get away from the beach areas," Bree said.

"The problem is that everybody here has gone through hurricanes and they think they can handle them." John looked out at the crowd. "Hurricane parties can be fun but they can also be dangerous because people drink too much and don't take the precautions they should." He looked up and waved as Carris Nelson approached. "I think we should check with the weather bureau again."

"I already have," Carris said. "Lola's headed our way all right, but it'll be after midnight before she hits.

Meantime eat, drink and be merry because by tomorrow we may all be blown away." He smiled at Bobbie. "You look great, B. Lee. How about a dance?"

When Bobbie and Carris danced away, Dawn said, "She really does look good. What miracle have you wrought?"

"No miracle, Dawn. Bobbie's had a rough time and she's unhappy. She didn't want to come to the dance; I just helped her make up her mind."

"Is Miguel coming at all or is he too busy making sure everything's all right down at the dock?"

"He's busy, I guess." Bree didn't add that she hadn't seen or spoken to Miguel all day.

She and Dawn had just started toward the bar when Craig approached them. "Hi," he said. "How's this for a wingdinger of a hurricane party." Thunder rumbled and lightning shot through the room. Craig put his arms around Bree. "I'm afraid," he joked. "Protect me, beautiful."

Bree stepped out of his arms, but he took her hand and turned to Dawn. "Excuse us, will you? I'm about to dance with the lady.

"I haven't thanked you for helping me out the other night," he told Bree when they were alone. "It was above and beyond the line of duty and I'm grateful."

"You're welcome. Just don't do it again."

"I won't and that's a promise." He pulled her closer. "The music sounds good, doesn't it? This reminds me of prom night."

Bree smiled. "Yes, I do remember having one dance with you." She looked up at him. "Let's face it, Craig, you couldn't see me for dust. You were mad about Bobbie Lee."

"Don't remind me," he growled.

"But I want to remind you," Bree insisted. "You were in love with Bobbie way back then, Craig, and she was in love with you."

"Yeah, well, things happen. People change."

"But I'm not sure love changes." Over his shoulder she saw Carris and Bobbie. When they were closer to the couple she tapped Bobbie's shoulder and said, "Change partners."

Bree stepped into Carris's arms. As she glanced back she saw Bobbie Lee's startled look and Craig's frown. Then Craig looked at Bobbie Lee and his eyes widened. "You . . . you look wonderful," Bree heard him say.

"If I didn't know better I'd say you planned that," Carris said.

"Who, me?" Bree shot him a look of innocence just as another flash of lightning illuminated the room. "This is insane," she said. "We ought to get out of here and head for higher ground."

"Higher ground? You've been away longer than I thought, Bree. There *is* no higher ground in Key West."

"Then at least we should try to get everyone away from the beach."

"Why? The Beachcomber's been here forever. If it withstood the hurricane of 1935 it'll withstand this one. Besides, maybe old Lola'll wear herself down before she hits us." Carris looked around him at the dancing couples. "I'm afraid you'd have a hard time getting anybody to leave. This is the last night of the reunion and they're having a good time."

"I know, Carris, but—"

"It's going to be all right, Bree. We've survived other hurricanes—we'll survive this one."

She wasn't sure. Deep down inside she had a feeling of foreboding. But maybe Carris was right, maybe the Beachcomber was perfectly safe. It was still possible that the hurricane wouldn't be as severe as the weather forecasters feared.

Bree danced with other friends after that. After each dance she told herself that soon she would leave. Once or twice she saw Bobbie Lee and Craig. They were sitting at one of the tables near the dance floor. They were talking earnestly to each other the first time Bree saw them. The second time she saw them they were holding hands.

When the musicians took a break Bree went looking for Dawn. She saw Dawn and John at the bar, and just as she approached them John said, "I think we ought to stop the dance right now and get everybody to one of the shelters."

"I don't think they'll go," Dawn said. She looked up at Bree. "John thinks we should get everybody out of here. What do you think? The forecaster said the hurricane would hit us about midnight. It's only ten-thirty now. There's still time to get to a shelter if people want to leave."

Bree glanced around the room. "If we tell them to leave they'll only head up to somebody's room for a hurricane party."

"Damn it!" John looked angry. "That's stupid. They should be in a shelter, not getting drunk."

"Mr. Sobersides." Dawn laughed, then seeing how serious John was said, "If you say we ought to leave we will. Look, why don't we go outside and see what's happening? We can't tell anything in here."

"Okay." John took her arm, then turning to Bree said, "C'mon along. Let's have a look."

The three of them made their way through the ballroom and out to the patio. "The wind's picking up," John said. "It's going to blow all right."

Bree looked up at the sky and felt the first drop of rain on her face.

John put his arm around Dawn. "We're leaving," he told her. "Can we take you to your mother's, Bree?"

She shook her head. "She's not there. Antonio Rivas took her to his place. I'll go over there in a few minutes. You and Dawn go on, I've got a car."

"Are you sure you'll be all right?"

"Of course I will. It'll only take me a couple of minutes to change and pack a bag. I'll be out of here in thirty minutes."

But it was longer than that. When she went back into the ballroom Craig claimed her for a dance. "Bobbie and I have done a lot of talking tonight," he said. "We're going to get back together, Bree."

"Oh, Craig, I'm so glad," Bree said with a smile. "And tomorrow you'll see a doctor, won't you?"

"If Key West is still standing tomorrow, yes, I'll see a doctor. I told Bobbie about the way I felt, the fears I've always had about dying young, and she was wonderful." Craig hesitated. "We talked about the affair I had, too, Bree. That was hard, but I think she's been able to forgive me and put it in the past. And it *is* in the past, Bree, it won't ever happen again." He shook his head. "God, I've been such a fool. All I've thought about was myself, what I wanted, my own fears. I was so busy being afraid I didn't take the time to see how much Bobbie needed me." He looked over to where Bobbie was dancing with Carris. "She's beautiful tonight, isn't she?"

"Yes, she is." Bree looked at Bobbie and Carris, and at all the other couples who were dancing, husbands and wives most of them, the women in their new gowns, the men in their dinner jackets. Their faces were softened by the candlelight as they moved to the music. Suddenly Bree felt a lump rise in her throat because she wished she were dancing with Miguel.

Outside, over and above the sound of the music, she heard the wind, then before she could speak a gust hit the hotel. "Maybe we'd better ask the band to stop," he said.

Craig nodded. "I think you're right." He motioned to Carris and when the two couples were together he said, "The wind's really picking up. We'd better get everybody out of here."

"The band should be taking a break in a couple of minutes," Carris said. "I'll make the announcement then."

The four of them walked over to the bandstand. They waited a few minutes until the leader left the stage. Carris jumped up to the platform and clapped his hands. "Hey, everybody," he called out, "gather around."

It took a few minutes for all the conversations to stop. "Lola's starting to kick up her heels," Carris said. "Maybe it'd be a good idea if we called it a night and headed for a shelter."

Boos and catcalls followed the announcement.

A man Bree didn't recognize yelled, "Hell, Carris, the Beachcomber's been here for a hundred years or so. It'll still be standing after you and I are long gone."

"Yeah," somebody else said. "This is the safest place in town."

Gwen pushed her way through the crowd and ran up the steps to the platform. Facing the crowd she said, "I'm a member of the alumni committee that helped put this reunion together. I think everybody's entitled to vote on whether we stay and go on with the party or—" she looked scathingly at Carris "—or whether we slink off to a shelter."

A roar of approval went up.

"How many say we stay?" she yelled.

The room filled with cheers.

"And how many of you chickenhearted Conchs think we ought to head for the shelters?"

The few timid voices that were heard were drowned out by the boos.

"That's it," Gwen said. "I'd say the yeas have it."

"The hell they do!" a voice thundered from the doorway, and Miguel, dressed in a yellow slicker, his face wet with rain, elbowed his way through the crowd. He vaulted up to the platform beside Gwen. "The storm's hitting right now," he said. "We've already got a hundred-and-twenty-mile-an-hour gusts. It's getting worse every minute and ten-foot-high breakers are coming in over the seawall." He looked down at the crowd. "I know the Beachcomber's a great old hotel and that it's been here for a lot of years, but this is a dangerous storm. It—"

"It's not that dangerous," Gwen shouted. "If you're too chicken to stay—"

Miguel put his hands around her waist, lifted her off the platform and deposited her down on the floor. He saw Bree then and he saw Craig. But he didn't see Bobbie Lee, who'd been jostled away from them by the crowd. For a moment his face tightened and he looked away.

"There are plenty of shelters," he told the group. "I can't tell you what to do, but most of you are my friends and I don't want anything to happen to you. For your own safety you should get to a shelter." He looked at Bree again. Jumping down off the platform he faced Craig. "The storm's going to knock the hell out of us," he said. "Take Bree and get out of here."

"Miguel, wait . . ." Bree put a hand on the sleeve of his slicker but he pulled away from her and headed for the door. She ran after him and when she caught up with him said, "Where are you going?"

"What do you care? Your boyfriend's with you, he'll take care of you."

"Damn it!" Bree exploded. "Will you listen to me for a minute?"

"I haven't got a minute. I've got to get back to the dock. If the storm keeps up like this we could lose the boats."

She took hold of his arm again. "What about the *Lady Ann*?"

"We don't know. It looks bad." Miguel turned away from her, then hesitated and said, "Get out of here, Bree. Have Craig take you to Dad's. You'll be safe there."

She wanted to scream at him to listen to her but he'd already turned away and headed for the door. When he opened it a blast of wind tore it away from him before he could slam it closed himself.

Bree stared at the closed door, her eyes blurred by tears. When she went back into the room to find Craig and the others she said, "Miguel's right; we should leave while we still can."

Gwen, hands on her hips, glared at Bree. "I was born in Key West and I've lived here all my life," she said. "I'm staying and so is everybody else who isn't afraid of their own shadow."

Bree ignored her as she looked at Bobbie and Craig. "I'm going up and packing," she said. "Then I'm going over to the Rivas house. You're welcome to come if you want to."

Craig shook his head. "Bobbie and I are going to stay here tonight," he said.

Bree nodded. She thought Craig was wrong but it was his decision. She hugged Bobbie Lee and said, "You take care." Then she took the flashlight out of her evening bag and started toward the stairs.

The halls were dark and empty. Except for the growling howl of the wind there was no sound. Bree flashed the light in front of her, then to the doors to see the numbers. When she found her own room she unlocked the door and went in. She put the flashlight on the dresser so that she had enough light to see when she took her things out of the drawers. As quickly as she could she got out of her evening dress and put on the skirt and T-shirt and sandals she'd worn that afternoon before the party.

When Bree was ready she picked up the phone to call her mother. The line was dead. She jiggled the phone a few times then put it down. She was glad Antonio Rivas had taken Cornelia to his home where she'd be safe.

But what about Miguel? Would he be safe? Bree stood in the middle of the room. If it wasn't safe here at the Beachcomber what would it be like down on the docks? A blast of wind struck the hotel and Bree felt it shudder. She thought of the *Lady Ann*, of Miguel alone down by the water, and she knew she had to go to him.

She picked up her bag and headed out of the room.

Rain slashed against Bree's body as she ran from the hotel. She staggered, almost knocked off her feet by the force of the wind, and held her hands in front of her face to protect herself from the flying debris.

Palm trees bent almost to the ground, falling leaves and palm fronds whipped past her as she ran toward her car. She gasped when she saw that a tree had fallen and crushed the car next to hers.

Bree wrenched the door of her car open and got inside. She hadn't realized, hadn't even imagined the storm was already this bad. She stared unbelieving at the fury around her and her hands tightened on the steering wheel. Then, her face set and determined, she started the car and backed out of the parking lot.

The beams of her headlights stabbed through the dark streets. Every blast of wind threatened to overturn the car and she fought to keep it on the road. When she switched the radio on, the newscaster said, "...of one hundred and thirty miles an hour are hitting Key West and the Keys. Ten- to fifteen-foot waves have been reported. If any of you listening out there haven't done so already, we advise you to go to the shelter nearest you. But if you don't go within the next fifteen minutes stay where you are. We'll stay on the air as long as we can to keep you posted on the storm. I repeat, winds of..."

Bree snapped the radio off. She peered through the black night, afraid of losing her way in the darkness. As she headed down toward the docks the wind grew even stronger. She bent over the steering wheel, trying to see against the palm fronds that slammed against the windshield.

She shouldn't have come out—she knew that now—but it was too late to turn back. For a moment a stab of fear ran through her body. What if Miguel wasn't there? What if he'd decided to go home?

After what seemed like an eternity, Bree pulled onto the docks. They were deserted. Through the darkness she saw the few buildings that housed the offices of other boat businesses. They were dark. She inched further down, toward the Rivas office. Oh, God, it was dark, too. Then she saw the flickering light of a lantern. "Thank God," she whispered.

Bree pulled as close to the building as she could. She got out of the car and the wind slammed her back against it, almost knocking the breath out of her. She gasped, then managed to close the door and bending low, ran toward the building.

The wind grabbed her, spinning her and knocking her to her knees. She sprawled, hands out, trying to find something to hold on to. But there wasn't anything. Rain lashed her body and a gust of wind caught and rolled her. She dug her fingers into the gravel of the parking lot, but the wind was too strong and she skittered on, skinning her knees as she clawed frantically for a handhold.

Her body thumped against something and pain jabbed her side. She realized she'd hit the cone-shaped speed breaks and grasped hold of them. A crack of lightning split the sky and in the sudden light she saw the docks and heard the terrible roar of the waves that crashed over them.

With a grunt of effort, spurred on by her fear, Bree got to her hands and knees. The Rivas office was close. She struggled toward it and cried out in relief when she reached the stair railing. She clung to it with both hands, sobbing as she began to inch herself upward, step by painful step.

She called out once to Miguel, but knew he couldn't hear her. The force of the wind grew stronger as she neared the top of the stairs. It battered the hands that gripped the railing and pulled at her body. Blinded by the rain, she screamed for Miguel, but her cries were lost in the wind.

Finally, her body battered and her clothes ripped, Bree reached the top of the stairs. She hung onto the railing with one hand and with the other beat on the door, calling out again.

Suddenly the door opened. She saw his startled face as he reached out for her. But her hand was frozen with fear onto the railing.

"Let go," Miguel shouted. "Bree, let go of the railing." He pried her fingers loose and carried her inside. He laid her down on a leather sofa and she clung to him, sobbing with relief.

"What in the hell are you doing here?" he said. "What in God's name possessed you to go out in this?" He held Bree close, his face against hers. "My God," he murmured, "you could have been killed."

Bree couldn't speak. All that mattered in the world now was that she was safe in Miguel's arms. She began to shake with reaction and he said, "Wait, let me get you some brandy."

He left her for a moment and when he returned he put his arm around her and held a glass to her lips. "Drink this."

The fiery liquid burned her throat but she drank it. "I'm all right," she managed.

"No, you're not." Miguel looked her over. "Your knees are skinned and you've got a nasty cut on your forehead and one on your arm." He helped her to sit up and unbuttoning her torn blouse said, "Let's get you out of these wet clothes, Bree. Then I'll have a look at those cuts."

"I'm okay," she protested.

"Don't argue with me." Miguel slipped the blouse off her shoulders. "Damn," he muttered, "you're all cuts and bruises. Hold on for a minute, I'll be right back."

When he returned—armed with a pan of water, towel, soap and alcohol—he bathed Bree's face and arms. He wiped her wounds with alcohol and put bandages over the most serious abrasions.

When he looked at her knees he whistled and shook his head. Before Bree could object he undid the fastening of her skirt and slid it down over her legs.

"I'm cold," she said with a shiver.

"I'll get you something to cover up with in a minute. First I've got to take care of your knees." He shook his head. "I'm sorry, Bree, this is going to hurt."

Bree looked down. Both knees were skinned and bloody. "Yuck," she said, then closed her eyes and tried not to flinch while Miguel, as gently as he could, cleaned the wounds.

"I'm going to put alcohol on them now," he cautioned.

"Sure. Go ahead." Bree took a deep breath, a breath that hissed through her teeth when the alcohol touched her.

Miguel closed a hand on her thigh. "Take it easy." He waited a moment. "Are you okay?"

"More or less." Bree's body quivered with reaction. "I'm cold," she said and hugged her body.

Miguel stood up. "I'll be right back." He hurried into the bathroom just off the office and when he came back he had one of his flannel shirts and a blanket.

He sat down next to Bree again. Before she could object, he unfastened the front snap of her bra. When it fell away he put the palms of his hands against her breasts. "You're so cold," he said.

Bree looked at him, wanting more than anything else in the world to throw herself into his arms. His hands were warm against her breasts but his dark eyes were veiled and remote.

Miguel let her go and slipped her arms into the flannel shirt. Then, not looking at her, he said, "Your panties are wet. Take them off, Bree, and I'll cover you up with the blanket."

The urge to draw her into his arms was almost more than he could stand. It didn't matter that he'd seen her with Craig, all he knew was that she had come to him and that she was hurt and cold.

He tucked the blanket up around her shoulders. Bree looked up at him and the breath caught in his throat. He swallowed hard. "I'd better call Dad on the marine radio and let him know where you are," he said.

Bree nodded and pulled the blanket closer.

He got up and went to the radio. In a few minutes Bree heard him say, "Tell Mrs. Petersen that Bree is with me. It's too late to leave now, we'll have to ride the storm out here." She heard the crackle of his father's voice, then Miguel said, "No, there's been no word from the *Lady Ann*."

When he said, "Over and out," he came back to Bree. Looking down at her he said, "That was a damn fool thing you did, coming here. What in the hell were you thinking of, going out in the storm that way?''

"You." Her voice sounded small and lost. "I was thinking about you. I wanted to be here."

A gust of wind hit the building and he saw her shiver. He wanted to put his arms around her but he didn't. "What about Craig? Where is he?"

"He and Bobbie decided to stay at the hotel."

"He and Bobbie?" Miguel raised one dark brow in disbelief.

"I went to see her today. She and I went to the dance together. Tonight she and Craig made up."

"So where does that leave you? Out in the storm?"

Bree looked at him. She stood up and holding the blanket around her she advanced. Nose to nose with Miguel, she said, "I tried to tell you but you wouldn't listen. What you saw the other night, what you *thought* you saw, just wasn't so. Craig was drunk, drunk enough to tell me that he was afraid he was dying."

"Dying?" There was scorn in Miguel's voice. "That's a different twist."

"He thought he was dying," Bree went on, "because both his father and his grandfather had died of heart attacks when they were his age. He's been too afraid to go to a doctor. I gave him hell about that and I helped him up to his room. I took his shoes and his jacket off and loosened his tie. He walked me to the door. He put his arms around me and—"

"Kissed you," Miguel said. "I saw him kiss you."

"A brotherly kiss, Miguel." Bree looked up at him. "That's all it was. That's..."

A howling blast of wind hit and shook the building and without thinking Bree threw herself into Miguel's arms. She buried her face against his shoulder and wrapped her arms around his back, holding him as though she'd never let him go.

For a moment Miguel kept his arms to his sides, then slowly he embraced her.

"I wanted to kill Craig when I saw him kiss you," he said against her damp hair.

"How could you think...how could you ever think I'd let him touch me after you and I...after what's happened between us?"

"I didn't think. I saw you with him and I went crazy. I'm sorry, Bree."

Another blast of wind hit the building. The walls shook and the floor shifted under their feet.

Bree tightened her arms around Miguel. "Will the building hold?"

"Of course it will." But Miguel's eyes were worried.

He sat down on the sofa and pulled Bree down beside him. He turned the portable radio on, and caught the announcer saying, "We're right in the middle of it, folks. We've got winds of one hundred and forty miles an hour, with gusts over one hundred and sixty." Miguel snapped the radio off. "We ought to try to get some sleep," he said.

Sleep? Bree stared at him as though he'd suddenly gone mad.

"This is going to last most of the night," Miguel said. "When we're in the eye of the storm I'll go out and take a look at what's been happening, but for now all we can do is sit tight."

He put an arm around Bree's shoulder and drew her closer. He'd assured her that the building would hold but he wasn't so sure that it would, not in the kind of wind they were having now. He was glad that Bree was with him, but more than anything in the world he wanted her to be safe. Right now he didn't give a damn about Craig, all he cared about was that she'd risked her neck by coming out in the storm to be with him.

A blast of wind rocked the building. Bree trembled and Miguel pulled her into his arms.

She started to speak, but he stopped her words with a kiss. He was so grateful to have her in his arms again—to have her lips part and soften under his.

He pressed her down on the sofa and covered her body with his, trying to be careful of her injured knees. He pushed the blanket aside and opened her shirt so that he could feel the softness of her breasts against his skin.

Wind slammed against the building and again it was rocked by the terrible onslaught. Bree tightened her hands on his shoulders. "Hold me," she whispered. "Please, Miguel, hold me."

His body was a haven against the storm. He kissed her with a ferocity that sent waves of heat coursing through her veins. Thunder cracked and lightning streaked through the room. Bree cried out in fear but he took her cry into his mouth and rocked her to him, holding her so close she could feel the beat of his heart against her breasts.

He let her go long enough to pull off his jeans and kick them aside, and pressing her back to him he warmed her with his body. He kissed her breasts and rubbed his face against them, feeling her wonderful satin-like skin. Then he caressed her with his hands in just the way she liked, pinching her nipples erect so that he could take each one between his teeth to lap and stroke with the warmth of his tongue.

Bree clasped his shoulders. Nothing else mattered now—neither the storm raging outside, nor the waves that crashed over the dock and threatened to sweep them out to sea. This was all that mattered, the wild sweetness of being in Miguel's arms.

When he raised himself over her Bree looked up at him. The building shook and the walls that surrounded them creaked ominously. "Don't be afraid," Miguel said.

"I won't be," she whispered. "Not as long as you're with me."

"I'll always be with you, Bree." Then with a sigh Miguel joined his body to hers.

His movements quickened with the wind that raged around them; he shuddered as the building shuddered. He rocked Bree to him and told her how beautiful she was and how much he loved her. He caressed the curve of her waist and her back. He cupped her buttocks to urge her closer, then claimed her mouth again.

"Darling," Bree whispered. "Oh, darling."

His cadence quickened and the breath came fast in his throat. He called her name and in the answering howl of the wind she responded and together, joined in love, they soared over and above the wind to that special place where only lovers dare to go.

The storm raged around them, but they heard only their own whispered words of love. At last they slept, safe in the comfort of each other's arms.

Chapter Twelve

They awoke to silence. Bree's first thought before opening her eyes was that the storm was over. But as she came more fully awake she realized they were in the eye of the storm—that eerie, silent heart of a hurricane—that would quickly pass and give way to the second swirling half where the wind would blow in the opposite direction, almost always more dangerous than the first.

She felt Miguel move beside her. "I've got to go out and take a look," he said. He rolled off the sofa, reached for his jeans and turned the radio on. "We're in the eye of the storm. Don't go out. I repeat, do not go out. This is only the eye. It could last ten minutes or two hours. The storm isn't over, it will resume. I repeat, do not go out."

Miguel reached for his sneakers as Bree sat up and said, "I'm going with you."

"Oh, no, you're not."

She stretched, wincing in pain at the stiffness of her knees, and got up gingerly, pulling on the shirt as she went to the bathroom for the rest of her clothes. She came back, hopping on one leg as she put a sandal on. Before Miguel could say anything she kissed him. "Whither thou goest," she said.

He looked at her and shook his head. "Okay, but the minute I tell you to head back here you do as I say."

Bree saluted. Then she linked her arm in his and together they stepped outside—to a scene of terrible destruction. Trees had been blown over, wires were down. A trailer office had been picked up and deposited upside down some sixty feet from its foundation. Windows were blown out of buildings, wooden structures had been tumbled over on their sides, pieces of wood from them stacked like kindling against the palm trees. Roofs had blown off other buildings. A thirty-foot cabin cruiser lay on its side next to the Rivas office. Bree's rental car was upside down against a coconut palm. The scene was almost impossible to believe and for a moment she wished she had her camera.

Shaken, Bree reached for Miguel's hand. She looked up at him and he said, "I've got to check the boats."

The dock was intact but half the pier was gone, dangling in the sea like a skeleton with a broken back. One boat lay half sinking in the water. Another had been smashed against the dock. Miguel broke into a run. As he drew closer to where the Rivas shrimp boats were moored, someone hailed him from the *Dipsy Doodle*.

"Yo, Miguel!" Captain Bob called out. "Wanna go fishin'?"

"Jesus!" Miguel exploded. "What in the hell are you doing here?"

"Rode out the storm on my boat, boy. Hadda make sure she was all right."

"You crazy old coot!" Miguel tried to suppress a grin. "You could have been killed or washed out to sea."

"Sure I coulda, but I wasn't." Captain Bob smiled at Bree. "Mornin', miss." And to Miguel he said, "I gave a quick check; all the boats in our fleet are okay. Rode out the wind real good." He shook his head. "But this sure is some whomp-dinger of a storm." He ran a hand through his beard. "Any word from the *Lady Ann*?"

"No." Miguel shook his head. "Maybe she pulled in somewhere. If she could get into Graveyard Creek she'd be all right."

"But you don't think she did, do you, boy?"

"No, I don't."

Captain Bob looked out over the water. In a voice so low Bree could barely hear him he said, "There's worse ways to go, I reckon." A sudden puff of wind ruffled his beard. "The calm didn't last long, did it? You better get the young lady inside. It's fixing to start up again."

"Come back to the office with us."

"Nope, I can't do that. I'm going to stay right here. You go on now, I'm keeping an eye on things here."

"Damn it, Captain Bob—" But the captain had already turned and disappeared below.

"Can't you make him come with us?" Bree asked.

"I'm afraid not. He's been a fisherman for fifty years. The sea's his home, Bree. If he wants to stay I can't stop him. You get back to the office. I want to check on the other boats."

"But—"

"No argument. I said I'd let you come along if you'd go back when I told you to. I'm telling you now. Go back. The wind is starting to pick up; I don't want to worry about you."

"All right, Miguel. But please, don't be too long."

"I won't," he said as he turned away and sprinted down the dock toward the line of Rivas boats.

Bree went back toward the offices. She looked around, found a Sterno stove and fiddled with it until it lighted. Then she filled a pan and began to heat water for coffee. On the top of a file cabinet she found a bag of croissants. She picked up the phone, knowing it wouldn't work but still feeling the need to try. It was as dead as she'd imagined.

When the wind began to blow harder she went to the door and looked out at the destruction all around her. A chill of fear ran through Bree's body—fear for her mother, Miguel's family, and for all of her friends who'd stayed at the Beachcomber last night.

There was no sign of Miguel. She went back into the office when the marine radio came alive with voices calling the Coast Guard for information or help.

"Mayday, Mayday, this is *Lazy Days* calling Coast Guard," a garbled voice said. "I'm in the Tortugas near Bird Key Harbor. Situation serious. Taking on water...position is latitude..." The voice faded.

Another took its place. "Mayday. Mayday. This is the *Sea Maiden*. Five miles out of Boca Chita. Boat listing badly. Mayday. Mayday..."

There were other calls for help. Bree stared helplessly at the radio, listening to the desperate voices. As the wind began again she went to stand in the door and looked out at the roiling sea. Giant waves crested and broke over the dock, smashing hard in the growing force of the wind. Where was Miguel? Oh, God, where was he? Why didn't he come back?

He came at last, his hair blowing wild in the wind that almost tore the door from his grasp. "The boats are okay," he said.

"What about *Straight On Till Morning*?"

"I put her in dry dock as soon as the storm warnings went up." The radio cracked and he said, "Has any news been coming in?"

Bree nodded. "All of it bad. My God, Miguel, those boats out there. How can they survive? How can...?" She hugged her arms. "I don't think I ever realized how terrible a really bad hurricane could be—not until now."

Miguel put his arms around her. "I shouldn't have let you stay. I should have taken you to my dad's during the lull."

"No." Bree burrowed close to him. "There wasn't time. Anyway, I wouldn't have left you."

He tilted her face for a kiss. "I'm glad you've come back," he said. "I'm sorry for what I thought. I should have known—"

"Shh. It's all right. I understand, Miguel—at least now I do. It was prom night all over again, wasn't it?"

He held her away from him as he took a deep breath and said, "How did you know?"

"My mother and I had a talk." She smiled and handed him a cup of coffee. "She always liked you. I didn't know that—it surprised me."

"Just about as much as it surprises me."

"She said she could see how much you liked me when we were back in school, and I guess that frightened her. She was afraid that you'd...that we..." She grinned up at him. "You know."

"Yes, I know. She was right. I wanted you so bad back then my teeth used to ache." He kissed her, hard. "My teeth are aching now, Bree."

She stepped away from him and giving him a croissant said, "Here, you need your strength." She tried not to flinch when a gust of wind shook the building.

If anything, this part of the storm was even worse than the first. During the hours that followed they sat together on the sofa, listening to the howl of the wind battering the building. A shutter blew off and through the glass Bree could see the storm at its ferocious worst. Before Miguel could stop her she ran to the window for a closer look, and gasped at the waves that lashed over the dock and the breakwater began to creep inch by inch into the yard and up the stairs to the office.

"The water's rising," she said, "it—"

Miguel grabbed her. Without a word he shoved her into the middle of the room—just as the window crashed in, scattering glass, smashing the Venetian blinds against the wall.

"Stay down!" he ordered as he ran to gather up newspapers to stuff into the shattered window. Quickly he grabbed a board from behind the file cabinets. "There's a hammer and nails in the bottom cabinet," he called to Bree.

When he'd nailed the board in place he said, "Are you all right?"

"Yes." Her voice was shaky. "It's worse than anybody thought, isn't it?"

Miguel nodded. He took her hand and led her to the sofa. "It can't last much longer, Bree."

"But it's been going on for hours." She looked at him. "Do you think the hotel is all right? All those people... My God, Miguel, what if something happens to the hotel? You tried to warn them. You told them to leave but they wouldn't listen." Tears streaked her face. "What if your dad's house isn't safe? My mother..." She couldn't go on.

"The house is safe, Bree. Believe me, my father won't let anything happen to her." He put a finger under her chin to lift her face and carefully wiped her tears away with his thumb. "I'll tell you a secret. I think Dad's got a very special feeling for your mother."

Bree's eyes widened. "What kind of a feeling? They've never gotten along. Mother's always called him 'that man.'"

"Well, 'that man' has had a thing for your mother for the last three or four years."

"You're kidding!"

"Nope." Miguel laughed. "You should see the expression on your face."

"He sent her roses." The way Bree said it, it sounded like an accusation. Then she punched his arm. "I thought they were from you." She sat up and pulled away from him. So much had happened in the last twelve hours that she'd forgotten about the young woman she'd seen him with here in his office. "Who was she?" Bree demanded.

"What? Who? What're you talking about?"

"The brunette who was here in your office? *Hugging* you?"

"Her name is Gabriela Ruiz." Miguel grinned. "She's my third cousin."

"Once removed?" Bree glared at him.

"Gabby's been hanging around for years. She followed me over here after the party at Dad's. There's nothing between us, Bree. She's a kid."

"Some kid!" A blast of wind shook the building and she grabbed Miguel's hand.

"Come here, Bree." He folded his arms around her and kissed the top of her head. Then he tilted her face for his kiss. "There's nobody but you, Bree," he said against her lips. The kiss deepened and he tightened his arms around her.

They made love again, there in the pallid darkness of the room while the wind howled all around them and the sea raged ever closer. Miguel held her and told her how beautiful she was and how much she meant to him. He kissed her again and again and when their bodies joined he told her he loved her in a voice that rose above the sound of the wind.

She forgot the storm that raged around them, the wind that clawed at the fragile structure. She was lost in Miguel's embrace, safe in the arms that held her, protected by the body that covered her. In that final moment she cried out in joy and joined with him in a defiant celebration of love that was stronger than the storm.

They slept and when they awoke the winds had ceased, the seas had stilled.

"I'll check on Captain Bob and take a look at the boats," Miguel said. "Then we'll go to Dad's." He kissed her. "This is one hurricane I'll never forget,

Bree.'' He held her away from him. ''Your mother was right, you know. I fell in love with you a long time ago. But I was a fool then, I let you go. I'll never let you go again.''

''Miguel...'' Bree looked up at him, a mixture of emotions in her wide green eyes.

''No.'' He shook his head. ''No, don't say anything now. We'll talk about it later.''

Later. Bree nodded, then not quite meeting his gaze, she dressed and followed him outside.

Most of the trees were down all along the street where Antonio Rivas lived. Shutters had been blown off windows and two houses had lost their roofs.

Bree twisted her hands together in her lap. ''There's so much destruction,'' she said as she leaned forward, trying to see the Rivas house at the end of the street. When she saw it she gasped—a tree had fallen and smashed through the roof on the right side of the house.

Too frightened to speak, she could only point.

''Dios!'' Miguel sped toward the house and with wheels screeching pulled into the driveway.

Bree was out of the car almost before it came to a full stop. Before she reached the steps her mother ran outside. ''Bree! Bree! Oh, thank God!''

Cornelia held her close. Over Bree's shoulder she said to Miguel, ''We were so worried. Antonio tried all night to reach you on the marine radio. Are you all right? What about the shrimp boats?''

''There's some damage but not as much as I expected,'' Miguel said. ''Most of the dock has taken a terrible beating.'' He looked up to where the tree had fallen on the roof. ''You look as though you got it worse than we did. What—'' He paused as his father came out on the porch.

"Here you are at last!" Antonio grabbed Miguel in a bear hug. "*Por Dios*, I didn't sleep a wink worrying about the two of you." He put his arm around Bree. "And you, *muchacha*. I'm glad to see the storm didn't blow you away. What were you thinking of, going out in the storm that way? You could have been killed! Your mother was frantic when Miguel called us. Why did you do it?"

"I wanted to be with Miguel," Bree said simply. She gestured to the roof. "Was anybody hurt? What about Lupita and the aunts?"

"They're all right."

Antonio looked up at the second story of the house. "But it sure scared the hell out of us when that tree fell. It came right through the ceiling of the bedroom where Nellie was sleeping."

Bree looked at her mother—amazed that she didn't flinch at the pet name.

"When I ran into the bedroom I couldn't even see her; she was buried somewhere under the tree. Rain was blowing in and there was plaster all over everything. I thought I'd lost her until I saw her trying to break through the branches. I got them off her, got her out of bed and carried her back to my room." He took Cornelia's hand and gripped it tightly in his. "She was soaked to the skin and her nightgown was half torn off her. It's a miracle she wasn't hurt."

Bree stared at her mother, too shocked to speak. Cornelia's nightgown had been torn half off her? Antonio had put her in his bed?

Cornelia saw the look and her face flooded with color. "Well," she said, "well, my goodness I'm per-

fectly all right now. Why don't we have some breakfast? I'm sure the two of you are starved. Come on in.
Lupita's in the kitchen. The electricity is off but we
have a Sterno stove. There's ham and eggs and
grits . . ." She turned and fled into the house.

Bree looked at Miguel. She saw the amused look in
his eyes and shook her head in disbelief, wondering
what had happened here last night.

The portable radio was on when they went into the
house. The storm had wreaked havoc all along the
Keys before it had veered and slammed into the west
coast. Fort Myers, Estero and Naples had been hit
hard. Now the storm had turned out into the Gulf and
was headed for Tampico, Mexico. Damage was esti-
mated to be in the millions of dollars. Hardest hit had
been the hotels and residences along the beach. There
were no exact counts yet, but thirty-five people had
been reported killed and many others were missing or
unaccounted for.

Bree looked across the table at Miguel. "I've got to
get to the Beachcomber," Bree told him.

"I'll run by on the way to the docks," he said. "I'll
let you know what's happened there."

Bree shook her head. "No, I want to see for myself. I'll take Mother home. I've got to change and
start getting pictures. My editor will have my head if I
don't send back a story—he knows I'm down here.
And I've got to do something about getting a car."

"Take mine," Lupita said. "I'll stay here and finish mopping up."

"I'll help you," Cornelia said as she began to clear
away the dishes. "You let me know if we have any
damage at home, Bree. I'll tend to it later."

"There's no need for you to be cleaning up here, Nellie dear." Antonio put his arm around her waist. "You've got your own home to worry about."

"I'll worry about it when we've finished here."

"All right, then. You stay till I get back and I'll take you home." He kissed her on the lips. She blushed, then patted his cheek. "Be careful," she said.

Bree felt as though the world had turned upside down. Her mother—straitlaced, straight-backed Cornelia Petersen—had not only allowed someone to call her Nellie dear, she had allowed that same someone to kiss her. What in the world had happened last night?

She looked at Miguel. He raised one eyebrow and said, "I'll see you later, Bree." He started out the door, then turned back for a moment. "Be careful where you go, both driving and walking. There's a lot of debris. I know you want pictures but don't take any chances."

When both men had driven away in Miguel's pickup, Bree said, "I'd like to see the room where the tree fell—would you mind showing it to me, Mother?"

"No, of course not. Just let me finish up here."

But Lupita shook her head. "You go on up with Bree, Mrs. Petersen. I'll finish in the kitchen."

Bree was silent as she followed her mother up the stairs. Cornelia led her down the hall, and opened a door.

Bree gasped. The floor of the bedroom, as well as the bed, was covered with plaster and water, leaves and broken branches. The bed had collapsed from the weight of what looked like most of the tree.

"My God!" Bree said. "You could have been killed!"

Cornelia nodded in agreement. "I was asleep when it happened. For a minute I thought the house had blown in all around me. There I was in bed with a tree! I couldn't move, all I could do was scream. Then the door burst open and Antonio ran into the room. He started yelling in Spanish and just…just clawing at the tree until he got me out from under it. Then he *swooped* me up into his arms and carried me down the hall to his room."

"His room?" Arms crossed over her chest, Bree looked at her mother, trying to come to terms with the situation. She was genuinely happy for her mother— it just all seemed so sudden.

Cornelia's cheeks were on fire. "Shall we go downstairs now?" she said breathlessly.

Without a word Bree followed Cornelia out of the ruined bedroom. When they were in the kitchen Lupita handed the keys to her car to Bree.

"When would you like to have it back?" Bree asked.

"There's no hurry. I'll be here most of the day. Just be careful—not of the car but of you."

Bree smiled her thanks, then turned to say goodbye to her mother. It was an awkward moment. She felt uncertain, but then her expression softened and she put her arms around her mother. All that mattered was that her mother had come safely through the storm and that she seemed truly happy. If Cornelia really liked Antonio Rivas—and she gave every indication that she did—then Bree was happy for her. The thought of her mother and Antonio Rivas together was incongruous, but strangely right.

Ten minutes later she pulled up in front of her mother's house. Flowers and shrubs had been torn up and scattered over the usually neat lawn and some of the tile had blown off the roof. But other than that, there didn't appear to be any damage. There were a few trees down on the other side of the street, but compared to the other parts of town she'd just driven through, Eaton Street had gotten off relatively easily.

Nothing had been damaged inside the house, Bree noted as she ran up to her room. She took a quick shower and dressed in jeans and a sweatshirt. She grabbed two of her cameras, loaded them both, shoved extra film and a pad and pencil into her camera case and ran back downstairs and headed for the beach.

Almost immediately Bree started taking pictures. Telephone poles were down everywhere, cars had been overturned or smashed by trees. She drove down Whitehead Street. The Hemingway house and the Audubon house were still standing. All along Duval Street, the stores had been boarded up, but some of the boards had blown away and windows were shattered. There was a speedboat at the corner of Duval and Fleming. She stopped the car, took pictures, then headed for the beach.

Bree was all professional as she concentrated on the scene and the photos she took. When she drew nearer to the beach she slowed the car. The damage here was terrible and part of the road was blocked by fallen trees. Bree skirted around them but as she neared the Beachcomber she saw that the road had been roped off. She parked the car on the shoulder and ran halfway to the hotel before a uniformed guard stopped her.

"Sorry, miss," he said. "This is as far as you go."

"Sorry, miss," he said. "This is as far as you go."

Bree flipped open her wallet and showed him her press card. "*Our World Magazine*," she said. "Was the Beachcomber hit hard?"

"Yes, ma'am—a lot of people were hurt there. You be careful, hear?"

"I will. Thanks." Bree ran toward the hotel. From this angle it didn't look too bad; it was only when she got closer, toward the back of the hotel, that she saw the terrible devastation. Most of the tile roof had been blown off and debris littered the swimming pool. The arched corridor looked as though a giant hand had ripped it apart. The smaller trees in the garden were down and palm fronds and coconuts covered everything.

Bree's mouth went dry as she snapped dozens of photographs. This was worse than she'd imagined.

She put more film in both cameras and ran toward the hotel. Again she had to show her credentials to the guard at the door.

The water was almost knee deep as she struggled toward the lobby. God, everything was a mess! She shot three pictures and when she saw another guard she hurried to him and said, "What about the guests? Was anyone hurt?"

"Yes, ma'am, there were a lot of people hurt. The worst of them have been taken to the hospital but there're others in the Sea Bird Room, waiting for more ambulances to come."

"Okay, thanks." Biting her lip, her face tense with worry, Bree ran toward the bar. Through the open door she could see cots aligned against the wall. A nurse in a white uniform hurried to a bed at the end of the room; a young doctor bent over a patient.

Bree snapped a dozen pictures in rapid succession before she went to the nurse and said, "I beg your pardon. Where can I get a list of the people who were hurt last night?"

"The Red Cross has that information," the woman said as she stood up. She put a hand against her back and looking at the row of cots shook her head. "What's the matter with people? There was plenty of warning about going to shelters last night, but there was some kind of a big party going on in the ballroom and people wouldn't leave. They just kept on dancing and drinking until half the roof caved in."

"The roof caved in?" Bree had to hang on to a cot for support. "I was at the party," she said. "It was a high-school reunion. Most of my friends were there. Excuse me..." She turned away from the woman and moved quickly down the line of cots.

"Bree? Is that you, Bree?" A woman whose head was bandaged struggled to a sitting position.

"Frannie?" Bree hurried to the cot. "My God!" she said. "What happened? Are you all right?"

"I'm better than some. They took the most seriously hurt to the hospital." Frannie covered her eyes with her hands. "Oh, Bree," she groaned, "it was terrible. I was standing by the bar with Craig and Bobbie Lee when there was this terrible crash and..." She began to cry. "Everything just...just fell in, Bree. It was awful!"

Bree knelt on the floor and put her arms around Frannie. "What happened to them, to the others?" she asked. "Are they all right?"

"I don't know, Bree, not for sure. Jean's all right, I think—and Carris. But Gwen was hurt, I know because I remember seeing boards or something fall on her just before I fainted. Bobbie Lee's here. Craig's in the hospital..."

Bree held Frannie's hand as she looked down the row of cots. "I've got to find Bobbie," she said, "but I'll be back."

Bobbie Lee was in the fifth cot down from Frannie. Her eyes were closed but when Bree whispered her name the other woman opened her eyes and reached a hand out to Bree. Her other arm was in a splint and the lower part of her face was swollen.

"Jaw may be broken," Bobbie managed. "Wire it soon as I get to hospital. One way to lose weight." She winced in pain. "Craig?" she said. "Where's Craig?"

"I don't know, Bobbie, but I'll find out."

"Ceiling fell. Craig pushed me down. Covered me." Tears streaked Bobbie's face. "Don't know where he is, if he's..."

"Shh, Bobbie, don't try to talk. I'll go to the hospital and find out what's happened to him. If you're not in the hospital by then I'll come back here and let you know how he is." Bree looked up as a nurse approached. "How soon before more ambulances are available?" she asked.

"It'll be another hour or two, I'm afraid." She looked down at Bobbie. "How're you doing? I'm sorry about the delay, we're doing the best we can."

"I know." Bobbie reached for Bree's hand. "Find him," she said.

"I will." Bree kissed Bobbie's forehead, then she went back to Frannie to say goodbye before she left.

From the hotel, Bree drove out to the airport and expressed the rolls of film she'd taken to her editor in New York.

The man behind the counter in the express office assured Bree the package would be in New York the first thing in the morning. "Sure is a hell of a thing, isn't it?" he said conversationally. "Buddy of mine lost dang near everything he had last night."

Bree agreed that the storm had been terrible, then sprinted back to the car and headed toward the hospital. She would check on her friends there, she decided, then she would go down to the docks to take pictures and tell Miguel she was heading up to the other Keys.

A flash of excitement zinged through Bree's blood. The pictures she'd taken today had been good; her editor, Alex Henderson, would go wild when he saw them.

But suddenly, in the midst of the excitement, she thought of Miguel. He hadn't mentioned the future, but she thought that when this emergency was over he might ask her to marry him. She wasn't sure what her answer would be.

Her career had moved ahead this past year but she still hadn't achieved everything she wanted to. If she married Miguel she'd spend the rest of her life right here in Key West.

And, God help her, she didn't think she could do that.

Chapter Thirteen

It took Bree only a few minutes to find out what room Craig was in. "We're monitoring him," the doctor in charge told her. "He has a broken leg and his back is sprained, along with numerous lacerations and a minor concussion. But he's going to be all right. He keeps asking about his wife."

"I've just come from her," Bree said. "She's anxious about him, too. May I see him?"

The doctor nodded, then hurried down the hall to his other patients as Bree pushed the door open.

Craig's head was bandaged, his leg was in a cast and there were smaller bandages on his face and his arms. Bree held back a gasp when he turned and saw her. "I hope you're not as bad as you look," she said.

"I'm not." His voice sounded groggy. "Where's Bobbie? Nobody'll tell me anything."

"She's all right, Craig. I've just come from the hotel. They've set up cots in the bar and they're keeping some of the people there until more ambulances are available. It looks like her arm is broken and maybe her jaw." Bree gave him an encouraging smile. "She was joking that if they wired it shut, at least she'd lose weight."

Craig closed his eyes. "God, Bree," he said, "I've been such a damn fool. When everything came crashing down on us last night, all I could think about was what a fool I've been and how much time I've wasted. I've loved Bobbie Lee since I was a kid, and I left her. Last night I was afraid that time had run out on me and I'd never had a chance to tell her how I felt."

"You're going to have a lot of time," Bree said. "You'll have the rest of your lives." She hesitated. She didn't want to upset Craig but she was anxious for news of her other friends. "What about Carris?" she asked. "And Gwen? Frannie told me Gwen had been badly hurt."

"I don't know, Bree. When I woke up I was in the ambulance on my way here. Sorry."

"That's all right, Craig. I'll check on them." Bree kissed his cheek. "Before you leave the hospital I want you to consult a cardiologist. Will you promise me that?"

He managed a grin. "I promise," he said.

The nurse at the desk had no information about a Carris Nelson or a Gwen Bradford but she told Bree to check in emergency. The emergency room was filled. People were lying on stretchers or propped up in chairs, their eyes dazed, while they waited for someone to care for them.

Almost automatically, Bree focused her camera and began shooting pictures. When a harried nurse asked her what she thought she was doing Bree told her she was looking for two friends.

"You need a camera to do it?" the nurse asked sarcastically. "Go ask at the desk, the clerk there will have the names of anybody who's been admitted."

At the desk Bree was told that Carris had been dismissed and that Gwen was in surgery. When she left the hospital, she drove back to the Beachcomber to tell Bobbie Lee that Craig was all right but that he was worried about her.

As she was leaving the hotel another ambulance came and the nurse who'd been taking care of Bobbie assured Bree that both Bobbie and Frannie would soon be on their way to the hospital.

From the Beachcomber Bree drove down to the docks. Before she went to look for Miguel she began to snap more pictures—parts of boats that had washed in to shore; an orange life jacket had snagged on a piling; the end of the pier dangled in the water.

Bree climbed down onto a rock to get a better shot of a thirty-foot cabin cruiser that had smashed against the seawall. She focused on the name, *Liza Jane*, when she heard Miguel say, "They haven't found the bodies of the man and wife who were aboard when she went down yet. Maybe if you wait a while they'll wash in, too."

Bree whirled around, her eyes wide with shock. "What did you say?"

"I said you ought to hang around awhile so you'll get a better shot of any bodies that might wash in." Miguel looked at her—a look that cut to her heart—

before he turned away and started down the dock in the direction of the shrimp boats.

Bree stared at his retreating back, then climbed up on the dock and ran after him. Grabbing his arm she said, "What's the matter with you? I'm a photojournalist—I'm only doing my job."

"Your job?" Miguel glared at her. "Come on, Bree," he said caustically. "All this destruction and all you can think about is your damned job."

"It's what I have to think about," Bree said, as angry as he was now. "I take photographs for a news magazine and the hurricane is a big story—"

"A big story!" He pulled away from her.

"Yes, damn it. Like it or not, it is. I'm a photographer, Miguel. I'm doing what I'm paid to do."

"Then do it somewhere else."

Bree stared at him, unable to believe his words. She shook her head as though trying to clear it. "What is it?" she asked. "Why are you so angry?"

"We've just had a confirmed report. The *Lady Ann* was lost. I'm on my way to tell her captain's wife that her husband and his crew are dead." He took a deep breath as though to steady himself. "I'm sorry, Bree. But at the moment I find it just a little bit obscene that people are going to buy your magazine just so they can exclaim over pictures of this . . . this destruction—this incredible loss."

Bree put her hand on his arm. "I'm sorry about the *Lady Ann*, Miguel. And I'm sorry about the destruction. But I didn't cause it—I'm only recording it."

He looked at her for a long moment, then said, "Can't you see what's happened here? Don't you understand the human suffering this storm has caused?" His dark eyes raked her. "Or do you just see life through the lense of your camera, Bree? Is it easier that way? Being on the outside, looking in at life?'' He shrugged her hand away.

Bree watched him walk away. For a moment angry tears stood in her eyes. Then she stiffened her shoulders and lifted her camera.

She didn't see why Miguel's anger was directed at her when what he was really upset about was the devastation caused by the storm and by the loss of the *Lady Ann*. She was tempted to run after him, to try to make him understand. But her face tightened with an anger to match his. He ought to understand about her work; until he did they had nothing to talk about.

It was almost dark by the time Bree got all the shots she wanted in the dock area. She spoke to Captain Bob and took what she thought would be a great shot of him standing on the deck of his boat glaring out at the sea.

Finally Bree drove back. At the rental-car agency she reported the damage to her car and rented another one. From there she drove Lupita's car back to the Rivas home to pick up her mother. Antonio, who'd just come home, drove her to the rental office. He told Bree to be careful driving in the Keys and assured her that he'd take care of her mother while she was gone. He leaned in the car window, kissed Cornelia without embarrassment and told her he'd see her later that night.

Bree didn't comment on their way home. She liked Antonio and it was wonderful to see her mother so happy. But she found herself wanting to caution her mother to go carefully. The thought of discussing anything so personal with Cornelia held her back until they reached the house. While Cornelia busied herself making a pot of tea, Bree set the table.

After a moment's hesitation Bree said, "Don't you think everything between you and Antonio has happened awfully fast?"

"Antonio and I have known each other for years, dear," Cornelia protested.

"And all that time he's been 'that man'! That's not the way you think of him now, is it?"

A smile tugged at Cornelia's mouth. "No, I don't suppose it is. For years I've been telling myself he's opinionated and domineering and macho." Her eyes twinkled. With a blush she said, "I've decided I don't so much mind the way he is. And I guess maybe I'm the one who's been opinionated and domineering. But it took a tree falling on me to make me realize that."

Bree stared at her mother. "You're falling in love with him, aren't you?" she asked quietly.

"I guess I am." Cornelia covered Bree's hand with her own. "I loved your father," she said. "I never thought I'd love anybody else. But Antonio…Antonio makes me feel more like a woman than I've ever felt in my life."

"Has he said how he feels?"

Cornelia nodded. "Yes, he has, Bree. But I don't think I want to talk about that right now." She stood up. "Besides, if you're set on driving the Keys tonight you'd better get going. We'll talk about it when you get back."

Bree slowly went upstairs to pack, grinning at the thought of her mother and Antonio Rivas.

When she was ready to leave she said to Cornelia, "I'll be gone for a few days. I'll shoot pictures in the Keys then go to Miami and send them on to New

York. I'll call you as soon as the phones are working."

"I wish you'd wait until morning. I don't like you driving alone at night, especially now. Reports are that the damage has been bad all along the Keys. Islamorada was hit hard and so was Plantation, so you watch your step."

"I will, Mother."

"I know Miguel's busy but I wish he was going with you."

"Yes, so do I." Bree kissed her mother. "I'm happy you're happy," she said. "Antonio's a wonderful man." Then she carried her cameras and an overnight bag out to the car and headed for the Keys.

The next two days were a nightmare. Bree had been six years old when Hurricane Donna had whipped through Florida with winds of one hundred and fifty miles an hour. When she was older she'd seen pictures of the storm that had wrecked houses in Islamorada, Windley and Plantation Key, wiped out the boat docks at Fort Myers Beach and carried a house in Bonita Beach over a quarter mile from its original site.

But the photos she'd seen when she was a child hadn't prepared Bree for what she saw all around her now. She took hundreds of pictures as she moved up the Keys. She was doing her job—just as she'd told Miguel—and if she was to do a competent one she had to disassociate her feelings from her work.

That first afternoon she stopped in Matecumbe to take pictures of a mobile-home park that had been almost totally destroyed. There were people poking through the rubble, trying to find whatever belongings they could salvage. Bree focused her camera on a thin young woman who was picking through the remains of what had once been her home. The woman had an iron skillet in one hand and a battered toaster in the other.

A little girl tagged along behind the woman. Her blond hair was tangled and her dress was torn. In a tiresome singsong voice, she kept saying, "I want my doll. Where's Mary Nell? I want my doll."

The woman bent down. Bree focused her camera as the woman got on her hands and knees and began to dig through the rubble. Bree's camera clicked. The woman pulled out a doll. The camera clicked again when the woman handed the doll to the child. The doll had lost an arm and its head hung by a thread.

Click, click, click, went Bree's camera. The child looked at the doll and began to sob. Bree focused on the child's face, then on the face of the woman watching the child.

Suddenly the woman turned and looked directly into the camera. Her expression was one of outrage, of strength and of dignity. She stood up and smoothed her ragged cutoffs. "Come on," she said to the child. "Let's go find your daddy."

Bree didn't move. Remembering the accusation in the woman's eyes, she told herself that photographers over the world were doing the same job she was, and that there was nothing wrong with what she was doing—or with her life.

That night she stayed in Tavernier. She bought a hamburger and a carton of milk and took it back to the motel that was still without lights. She ate by candlelight and tried not to think of the woman and the child or of the pictures she'd taken today.

When she finished eating, she picked up the cameras to reload them for the next day's shooting. Bree frowned. Had Miguel been right? Were her cameras a way to distance herself from life, a way to be on the outside looking in without being wholly involved?

Bree sat in the semidarkness for a long time before she blew out the candle and lay down on the narrow bed. Was taking photographs of tragedy obscene? She balled her hands into fists and struck the mattress. No, damn it, it wasn't. She reported news with her camera. The photographs she'd shot today would tell people in other places what a hurricane was like. Yes, she'd shot pictures of human suffering, but how else could she tell the story?

It was a long time that night before Bree was able to sleep. When she did it was to dream of Miguel walking away from her.

He missed her with an ache he hadn't thought possible. As tired as he was after a fifteen-hour day repairing the damage caused on two of the boats in his fleet, Miguel found it almost impossible to sleep. His home—the home where Bree had spent only one night—seemed curiously empty. His bed seemed too big to sleep in and after tossing and turning for an hour he got up and went out to the living-room sofa.

He didn't know why he'd spoken to Bree the way he had, why the idea of her taking a photograph of a smashed-up boat had so enraged him. Boats were his life, the sea was his second home. Had he reacted with angry words because he'd felt betrayed by the sea? Because the sea had taken the *Lady Ann*?

Or had it been the sight of Bree suddenly becoming a self-sufficient professional who no longer needed him? He didn't know; he only knew that when she wasn't with him he didn't feel complete.

He loved Bree more than he'd ever thought it possible to love. He wanted her with a passion that went beyond words, but what he felt went beyond passion. He needed Bree the way he needed sunlight and air. He wanted to spend the rest of his life with her, to have children with her, to sleep and wake with her.

The thought, the *fear* that it wouldn't work out between them, chilled Miguel to the bone.

The next morning he went to see Cornelia. She led him into the kitchen where she insisted he sit down and have a cup of coffee and a piece of chocolate cake. "I baked it to take to your father's tonight," she said. "Lupita's cooking paella and I said I'd bring the dessert."

"I'm glad you and Dad are friends, even if it took a hurricane to get the two of you together." Miguel took a bite of the cake, not sure how to talk to this woman he'd always thought of as straitlaced and set in her ways, this woman who was obviously important to his father.

When she sat down across from him, he asked, "Have you heard from Bree?"

Cornelia shook her head. She stirred a teaspoon of honey into her coffee. "I didn't want her to go traipsing around the Keys alone. I wish you could have gone with her but I know you and Antonio have a lot of cleaning up to do here."

Miguel nodded. "Did Bree say exactly where she was going?"

"No, only along the Keys. I assume she'll go as far up as Key Largo, then head to Miami to send the film to that boss of hers in New York." Cornelia took a sip of her coffee. "Did you two have a falling out?"

"Not exactly. I was upset about her taking pictures of the storm. It made me angry because the destruction was so terrible and she seemed to be only interested in getting the perfect shot."

"It's her job, Miguel."

"I know that." He looked at Cornelia. "And I'm afraid of it."

Cornelia nodded. "Yes, I think I understand. You're in love with her and you want her to stay here in Key West instead of going back to Paris. That's it, isn't it?"

Miguel took a deep breath. "That's it." He put his hands around the coffee cup. "I lost her once," he said. "I don't want to lose her again."

"Then fight to keep her. Don't just run off like you did when you were eighteen."

A long moment went by before Miguel pushed his chair back. He took Cornelia's hand. "I'm going to go find her. Will you tell my father I'll be back just as soon as I can?"

Cornelia stood at the door when Miguel backed the pickup out of the driveway. He waved, then headed out to Highway 1.

At Marathon, Miguel stopped for coffee and found out that a woman photographer had been there yesterday. He hit Matecumbe at dawn and had a quick breakfast. At ten o'clock in the morning he pulled into Key Largo, but it was afternoon before he found Bree.

She was on the bay side of the Key, just down from Buttonwood, standing in a foot of water, taking pictures of a house that had been badly damaged, and of a ruined dock. A boat lay crossways upon the broken planks and part of the house was half submerged in the water.

Miguel didn't say a word. He waited until she'd finished and waded toward shore before he spoke. "Hello, Bree. I've been looking for you."

Her face was drawn and there were patches of fatigue under her eyes. She took a deep breath as though to steady herself. "Hello, Miguel. What are you doing here?"

"Looking for you." He offered a hand to help her out of the water. "You look tired," he said.

She shook her head. "No, I'm all right."

"Have you had lunch?"

"No, I will later. I've finished here. I've got to get the film in to Miami."

"You can do it in the morning. Why don't you rest here tonight?"

A frown marred her forehead. "No, I can rest later. I've got to get to Miami."

"Damn it, Bree..." Miguel stopped. "All right, get your gear together. I'll drive you in."

Bree looked at him, then away. "I can drive myself."

"No, you can't." He was angry now. "Where's your gear?"

"In the car." She faced him. "There's no need for you to drive me. It's only a little over an hour from here to the Miami airport."

He took the camera bag off her shoulder. "Come on," he snapped.

He followed her to the Winn Dixie parking lot. She got out of her car, still protesting. But Miguel refused to listen to her protests. She was exhausted—he'd be damned if he let her drive. He locked her car and taking her by her arm led her to his pickup.

Bree didn't speak until they were out of Key Largo and heading up Highway 1. "Why did you come?" she asked.

"I wanted to tell you that I was sorry about the other day. You were only doing your job, I understand that now, but I was upset about the *Lady Ann*. We'd just gotten confirmation from the Coast Guard that the boat had gone down. I've known her captain since I was a boy. He and his wife were friends of mine." He glanced at her. "I knew the people who owned the boat you were photographing, too. They were nice people—he'd just retired a year ago."

"I'm sorry." Bree put her hand on his knee. "But I—"

"Sure," he said. "You had a job to do."

They didn't talk after that. Miguel looked at her once and she was asleep, her head forward, her blond hair almost covering her face. Her hands rested on one of her cameras.

When he turned off to go to the airport he woke her. "Where do I go when we get there?" he asked.

Bree straightened up. Pushing her hair back from her face she said, "Atlantic Courier Express," and began to put rolls of film and the notes she'd taken into an envelope. When Miguel pulled up in front of the express office she said, "I'll only be a minute," and hurried into the office.

When she came back out she said, "Okay, we can head back to Key Largo now."

Miguel didn't answer. Instead he turned the pickup toward the Julia Tuttle Causeway. At Bree's questioning look he said, "We're going to get a hotel room over by the beach. You're going to eat something and get some sleep."

"No." Bree's face was set and angry. "I don't want to do that. I want to go back to Key Largo and pick up my car and go home. I want—"

"I don't give a damn what you want." He was as angry as she was now. "You've got to rest and we've got to talk. Any preference in a hotel?"

"No, but..." Bree glared at him. "Damn it, Miguel—" but she stopped when she realized that he wasn't paying any attention to her.

Twenty minutes later he pulled up in the driveway of the Deauville Hotel, told her to wait while he checked on a room then went inside. He liked the way registering as Mr. and Mrs. Miguel Rivas made him feel.

The room faced the ocean. As soon as they were inside Miguel said, "Why don't you take a shower? I'll call down for dinner. Anything special?"

"No." Bree averted her face as she opened her bag and took out a pair of silk pajamas. She told herself she didn't want to be here with Miguel, that he had no right to drag her to a hotel. She was furious with him for the things he'd said to her after the storm. She'd only been trying to do her job... She leaned against the wall of the shower and let the hot water beat against her body. Oh, God, she was so tired.

When she'd dressed Miguel handed her a tall gin and tonic and led her to the balcony. "It's cool now," he said. "I thought we'd sit out here."

Bree took a sip of the drink, sighing with pleasure as she put her feet up on the railing of the balcony and looked at the sea. It was so calm now that it was difficult to believe the way it had been only a few days ago.

As if reading her thoughts, Miguel said, "It's beautiful, isn't it? On a night like this it's hard to believe how dangerous the sea is."

Bree nodded. "I'm sorry about the *Lady Ann*. I know how hard that must have been for you."

"It was, Bree." He reached for her hand. "But I shouldn't have taken my anger out on you."

"No, Miguel. I understand. I must have seemed heartless. Maybe I am where my work is concerned. But in order to do my job right I have to distance myself—otherwise it would be too difficult." She hesitated. In a voice so low he could barely hear her, she said, "Maybe you were right. Maybe I am on the outside looking in at life. But it's...it's the only way I know how to get the shots." She looked at him. "If I want to capture human emotions I can't let the way I feel color what I have to do. I have to stay remote, removed from what I'm shooting."

"Your job is that important to you?" Miguel held his breath, waiting for her answer.

"Yes," she said. "Yes, it's that important to me."

They spoke little after that. When the waiter brought their dinner they ate out on the balcony. The sky darkened and the moon rose over the ocean. When Bree began to nod, Miguel picked her up and carried her into the room and over her sleepy protests he put her in bed.

She was already asleep when Miguel came in beside her but she sighed when he pulled her into his arms and felt his lips brush her temple. "Go back to sleep, Bree," he said.

Once in the night Bree awakened to the sound of the steady roll of the ocean. Her head was on Miguel's shoulder, his arms were around her. She kissed his shoulder and curling her fingers in the hair on his chest went back to sleep.

She dreamt she was drifting on a turquoise sea, floating on her back over the waves, carried by the gentle motion of the water. A wave broke over her body and slid slowly across her breasts in a warming caress.

"Bree?" Miguel's voice was a whisper against her skin.

She turned into his arms. "I'm dreaming," she said.

"Is it a good dream?"

"A lovely dream." Bree raised her face for his kiss and the dream became a reality of sighs and whispers, of touches and sweet caresses.

She was all his now, yielding herself to him, cupping her breasts for his kisses, murmuring her pleasure when he moved down her body to trail a line of fire across her rib cage, her belly, her thighs. Gently he nipped the tender skin there, soft little love bites all around her thighs, teasing her until her body took fire and she whispered, "Please, Miguel. Please, darling."

"Please what, my love?" His mouth was warm against her skin. "Please this? And this?"

Bree moaned with pleasure. She told him how she loved what he was doing to her and when it became too much he covered her body with his and held her, letting their passion wait while he kissed her mouth and told her how much he loved her. Only when the waiting became a sweet torture did he join his body to hers.

Bree kissed his shoulder as they began to move together, slowly at first, like the gentle roll of the sea at ebb tide. Then the cadence quickened. Like a storm it became hard and swift, rising, growing until it threatened to sweep them away. Bree whispered his name and lifted her body to his in a frenzied surge of passion. His hands tightened around her and he whispered his pleasure against her trembling lips.

They held each other for a long time as the first rays of the morning sun crept over the balcony into their room. "I love you," Bree said into the quiet of the room.

Miguel brushed the tousled hair back from her face. "And I love you. I always have, I always will."

She turned her face to his and he felt the hot tears against his cheek. "Why are you crying?" he said.

"I don't know." Her voice was muffled. "I don't know, Miguel."

But he knew. He knew that she was crying because soon she would go away—back to Paris, back to her job. Away from him. His arms tightened around her body. "I won't let you," he whispered against the tumble of her hair. "I'll never let you go." But he knew in his heart that he would.

Chapter Fourteen

Bree put the phone down just as Miguel came in from the balcony. "That was Alex Henderson, editor of *Our World*," she said. "I've got to go to New York."

"New York? Why? You've sent the pictures."

"I know, and I sent a few notes along with them, but Alex wants the whole story—from my viewpoint."

"But you're not a writer."

"I know that, Miguel. What he wants me to do is relate everything that I've seen, the way I felt during the storm and in the aftermath, to a staff writer. He thinks if the story is told through my own experience in the hurricane, along with the pictures I took, it will bring...in his own words...great immediacy to the story. He wants to know about the night of the storm, what I did and—"

The shadow of a smile crossed Miguel's face. "I hope you're not going to tell him *everything* you did that night." He crossed the room and put his hands on Bree's shoulders. "Although it might make for interesting reading."

He wanted to tell Bree not to go because he was afraid if she went she wouldn't come back. He wanted to tell her that he loved her and wanted her to stay here in Florida with him—to marry him and have children with him. His hands tightened imperceptibly. "How long will you be gone?"

"Two or three days, a week at the most. Alex said I could stay here a couple of more weeks to compensate for going to New York." Bree stepped away from him. "I've got to call the airport, Miguel."

He let her go. "Sure. I'll take care of the rental car. Maybe it's best to turn it back in."

Bree nodded. "I hate to leave you with the problem, but I'd appreciate it."

"It's no problem, Bree. When you fly back into Miami don't bother with another car. Catch a flight to Key West and I'll pick you up there."

"I will." She turned away from him to pick up the phone. The next flight to New York left in an hour and a half and she booked a seat. Then she threw the few clothes she'd brought with her into her overnight bag and ran into the bathroom for a quick shower.

When she finished, she dressed in her jeans and a long-sleeved shirt. "I look like a beachcomber," she said ruefully. "Look, tell my mother what's happened, will you? And could you please check on Craig and Bobbie Lee? Gwen was in surgery when I left the hospital, so see if you can find out how she is." Bree grabbed her camera bag and glanced at her watch.

"I'm sorry, Miguel but we've got to leave right now if I'm going to make that flight."

Without a word Miguel picked up her overnight case. She hadn't even gone yet and he'd already started missing her. What would it be like if she went back to Paris?

He looked at Bree when they were in the pickup and suddenly he felt hollow inside—as though she'd already left him. Her face was animated as she told him about Alex Henderson, and she leaned forward in the car as though already anxious to get to her destination.

"He saw some of my photographs in a small magazine," she said. "I was just beginning, taking pictures in my spare time while I was still modeling. I used to roam around the city, snapping everything I saw—the slums, the tenements, the graffiti in the subways, the lovely old brownstones. I love New York, Miguel. It's the most exciting city in the world."

"More exciting than Paris?" He tried to keep his voice level.

"Yes, yes, I think so. I love Paris, too, but New York's different." She laughed. "It's New York!"

Miguel's hands tightened on the wheel.

"Alex got in touch with me. He looked at some more of my pictures and hired me as a staff photographer. That's when I quit modeling. Three years later there was an opening in the Paris office and he offered it to me."

Bree continued, talking about New York and Paris, her job and the people she'd photographed. When they got to the airport she said, "Don't come in. I'm going to run. I'll try to call you in Key West tomorrow night if the phones are working by then."

Miguel got out of the pickup with her and handed her the overnight bag and the camera case. "Have a good trip, Bree."

"I will." She kissed him, then turned and ran into the airport.

Miguel watched her disappear into the crowd before getting back into the pickup and heading for Highway 1. He understood more clearly now why he'd been so angry when he'd seen Bree taking photographs after the storm. It hadn't really been because he'd known the couple who had drowned when the *Liza Jane* went down, or even because of the *Lady Ann*. He'd been angry because he'd suddenly realized that Bree had a career that was important to her, that she was a professional who loved what she did. And he was terrified her career would separate them.

Bree loved him. That was an absolute. But she loved her career, too. Her camera was as important to her as the sea was to him. He knew he could never leave the sea; he didn't think she could leave her job.

The hollowness inside Miguel persisted. He was lost without her and she'd been gone for less than an hour.

At Key Largo he drove her car to the rental agency and walked back to the Winn Dixie lot to his pickup and started the trip home. Always before, no matter how many times he drove this stretch of highway between Key Largo and Key West, Miguel had been taken by the sheer beauty of sky and sea. But he found no beauty in the drive today. It was as though the color had gone out of his life.

As soon as he arrived in Key West he went directly to Cornelia's to tell her that Bree had gone to New York and that she would call as soon as the phones were back in order.

From there he went to see Craig. Bobbie Lee, her jaw wired shut and her arm in a sling, sat beside Craig's bed holding his hand.

"Hi, Mike," Craig said when he saw Miguel. "How ya doing?"

"I'm okay. What about you?" Miguel rested a hand on Bobbie's shoulder. "Can't talk, can you?"

She shook her head and rolled her eyes.

"It's driving her crazy," Craig said. "I talk and she listens and writes me notes. Where's Bree?"

"She had to go to New York on business. She'll be back in a few days. How's Gwen? Have you heard anything?"

"She's got a broken hip and her face was pretty banged up. She's going to be all right but she'll have to have a lot of plastic surgery. Dawn and John were in a little while ago and they said it was pretty bad."

Miguel stayed a few minutes longer. It was obvious from the way Craig and Bobbie Lee looked at each other that they were going to patch up their differences. When he left, they were making plans for a second honeymoon. He was happy for them and felt like a fool for thinking there'd ever been anything between Craig and Bree.

During the next few days Miguel kept busy checking the damage to the boats and trying to straighten things out with the insurance company. The phones remained down so there was no word from Bree. Toward the end of the week the Coast Guard found the wreckage of the *Lady Ann* but there was no trace of her captain or crew. A memorial service was held that Sunday and Miguel stood on the dock next to the captain's wife while she and the families of the crew threw wreaths into the out-going tide.

Sunday night he returned to his home, feeling as discouraged as he'd ever been in his life. He sat for a long time on the patio looking at the water, thinking about Bree, wondering what she was doing tonight. It was hell not being able to talk to her. He went in once and picked up the phone, hoping for a miracle, but it was still dead.

The moon came up, diminished and fading, the last remnants of the full moon he and Bree had seen that night in Miami Beach. Miguel went to the promenade and looked out at the sea. He knew that he was behaving like a lovesick fool, acting as though he'd already lost her. Well, he hadn't, and he wouldn't—not without a damn good fight.

Yes, she had a profession, he understood that and he respected it. He'd seen her photographs—hell, he'd been collecting them for years—and he knew how good she was. He'd never ask her to give up what she did; he just wanted her to do it here.

Key West wasn't a back-roads village, it was a haven for people as artistic as Bree was. If men like Tennessee Williams, Ernest Hemingway, John Dos Passos, Hart Crane and Robert Frost had lived and worked here, why couldn't Bree? He realized she couldn't cover world events, but there were other kinds of photography.

Bree loved the water as much as he did—perhaps she could do a book of photographs of the sea, of the islands in the Caribbean. They'd sail to Cancun and she could photograph the Mayan ruins at Chichen Itza and Tulum.

Tomorrow he would get the *Straight On Till Morning* out of dry dock. He would make sure everything was shipshape and stock her for a two-week cruise.

Bree had told him her boss was giving her an extra two weeks' vacation. That gave him two weeks to try to convince her that she could be happy here in Florida.

They'd head down to Andros or Eleuthera, maybe to Great Exuma. Miguel's hands tightened on the railing. He heard the roll of the ocean and thought of being alone there with Bree, of all the lazy days in the sun, of the quiet nights when they'd pull into a cove or an inlet. He thought of moonlit nights out on the deck with her, of making love to the gentle rocking of the boat and waking up with her in his arms.

Looking out at the sea he prayed that she'd come home.

Bree stared at Alex Henderson in shock. "You want me to go to Rome?"

"Sy Sommerlot is leaving next month," the large man who faced her across his desk said. "It'd be a big break for you, Bree, a hell of a lot more challenge than the Paris office. You'd be in charge of the Italian edition of *Our World*. It'd be your baby. You'd make the assignments and do the ones you really want to do. If you want to do a story in Venice or Florence, or even all the way down in Sicily, you don't have to check with anybody. It'd be your beat." He leaned back in his chair and grinned at her. "What do you say, Bree?"

"I . . . I don't know."

"What do you mean, you don't know? You'd be head honcho at one of the biggest magazines in Italy with a salary that'll have you sitting on top of the world. You've earned it because of these pictures."

Henderson pointed to the glossy prints he had spread out on his desk. "These are classics, Bree." He picked up the picture of the woman in Matecumbe going through the rubble of what had once been her home. "This is wonderful stuff. You deserve this promotion."

"I'd have to go home first. Everything's there. My clothes..." She shook her head. "This is so sudden, Alex. I have to think about it."

"Think about it? Are you kidding? Half the photographers on the staff would jump at the chance I'm giving you and you've got to *think* about it?"

"I didn't mean that the way it sounded, Alex. I'm sorry. It's just that . . . I'm tired, I guess."

"Sure you are. I know you worked damn hard after the hurricane." Henderson stood up. "I appreciate your coming to New York on such short notice, Bree, but the fact that you were there, at the scene of the hurricane, and that you used to live in Key West, rounded out the story."

Henderson came around the desk and draped his arm over her shoulder. "I told you on the phone you could take an extra two weeks but I've got to pare that down to one. Go back to Key West and take it easy for a couple of days. But call me—that is if they ever get the phones working. Beats the hell out of me why anybody'd want to live in a burg like that." He squeezed her shoulders. "On your way out stop in accounting. There's an envelope there for you with a nice fat bonus in it."

Bree thanked him and said that she'd call from Key West as soon as the phones were working or she made up her mind, whichever came first.

Rome! What an opportunity! She would love living there. Learning Italian wouldn't be too difficult. She was good at languages; she learned passable

French in six months and in a year she'd been practically fluent. The same with Spanish, but that had been easy. Because of the large Cuban population in Key West she'd had plenty of opportunity to practice while she was in school.

The Cuban population. Slowly her enthusiasm about the promotion drained away as Bree thought of Miguel. If she took the job in Rome that would be the end of their relationship.

When she first knew she cared about Miguel, Bree had thought that if she went back to Paris they would still see each other once in a while. She knew now that wouldn't work—that Miguel would never settle for a week at Christmas or two weeks in the summer. For him it would have to be all or nothing.

Nothing. Bree stared out the window of the taxi taking her back to the Plaza. How could she even think about leaving Miguel? But, as Alex had said, Rome was the opportunity of a lifetime.

That night Bree had dinner alone in her room. She made a reservation to fly to Miami the following afternoon, then tried to call Key West. The phones were still out. The next morning she went to Saks to buy a dress for her mother. She found a pretty pale green silk that she knew would look good on Cornelia, but hesitated because the style was a bit more daring than anything Cornelia had ever worn. "I'll take it," Bree told the saleswoman. Cornelia had already dared far beyond what Bree had ever expected; the dress would suit the new aspects of her personality.

When Bree left the store she walked up Fifth Avenue past Rockefeller Center. She paused in front of a nautical shop and looking in the window saw a captain's hat inscribed with the words, "Straight on, mate.'' She bought it for Miguel and when she left the shop—still thinking about him—she went into a bookstore and bought a copy of *Peter Pan*. Perhaps she'd read it on the plane.

But on the plane Bree sat next to an elderly gentleman who talked all the way to Miami. For the moment, at least, she forgot about the book.

As soon as the plane landed she made arrangements for a flight to Key West, then found a phone and tried to call Miguel at the office on the dock. He answered on the first ring.

"I can't believe the phone's actually working," Bree said.

"Just since this morning. Where are you?"

"In Miami."

"How soon will you be here?"

"I've got a flight in a few minutes. I'll get in at six."

"I'll be there."

"Call my mother, will you?"

"She and my dad are out somewhere for dinner." Miguel hesitated. "If I call her I'll have to take you back to Eaton Street," he said.

"Oh." Bree smiled at the phone. "Well, if my mother has a dinner date tonight..." She drummed her fingers on the phone stand. "I guess I could put the call off till morning." She took a deep breath. "Miguel, I've...I've got something to tell you. I'm—" The loudspeaker called out an announcement. "That's my flight," she said. "I've got to run."

"Okay, Bree. See you soon." Miguel frowned when he put the phone down. There'd been something in Bree's voice, excitement and a hesitation that seemed to warn that she was going to tell him something he might not like to hear.

He was at the airport when Bree's plane came in. She got off wearing a classic black linen suit and a small black hat. Very New York. Her hair was up and her long legs were clad in sheer black hose and her feet in high-heeled black pumps. She looked beautiful, classy, and very different than the woman he'd dropped off at the Miami airport a week ago.

When Bree saw him she ran toward him, the camera case bumping against her hip, the overnight bag clutched in one hand, a box from Saks in the other.

"God, it's hot," she said. "I'd forgotten how hot it would be here." She made a face as she blew at a loosening strand of hair. "It's autumn in New York. The leaves are turning. It's beautiful there now, my favorite time of year."

"Any more bags?" Miguel asked soberly.

"No, this is it."

He led her out to the car. "I'm glad you're home, Bree," he said.

"Me, too. I missed you."

"Did you?" He started the car and headed for the beach. "I thought we'd eat in if that's all right with you," he said. "Miranda—my twice-a-week chief cook and bottle washer—left fried chicken and potato salad in the refrigerator. Sound all right?"

"It sounds wonderful." Bree rested her hand on his thigh.

The hand on his leg warmed and excited Miguel. He felt a flame start in his belly and snake down to his loins. All the pent-up emotion, all the wanting he'd held in check this last week boiled inside him. He felt himself grow with need and it took every bit of will power not to pull off the road into the mangroves and take her right here on the front seat.

Miguel clamped his bottom lip with his teeth as Bree unconsciously began to rub his leg while she talked about New York, the friends she'd seen there and the shows she'd gone to. She crossed her long slim legs and he forced himself to look away.

When he pulled into his driveway Bree got out of the car. Once out of the air-conditioning she took her hat off and fanned her face.

He wanted to touch her but he didn't think he should, not now. "Maybe you'd like to change into something cooler, one of my T-shirts."

"No, this is all right. I'll just take the jacket off." She followed Miguel into the coolness of the house and accepted his offer of a drink.

He brought the drinks into the living room and handed Bree hers. "Cheers," he said.

"I have a lot to tell you."

"Have you?" Miguel looked at her and suddenly he was more afraid than he'd ever been in his life. He knew that he didn't want to hear whatever it was. He put his drink down on the coffee table and taking her hands he brought her to her feet.

"Miguel . . . ?"

"No," he said. "Not now. I don't want to talk now." He kissed her. "I've missed you," he said against her lips. Before Bree could speak he swept her up into his arms and carried her into the bedroom.

He put her down and pulled her into his arms, holding her so close he could feel the beating of her heart. He pressed kisses all over her face and spreading his fingers against her hair, he tilted her head so that he could kiss her throat and the soft skin behind her ears.

She whispered his name and her voice trembled and broke.

He opened her white satin blouse and pushed it aside so that he could touch the softness of her breasts through the wisp of white lace. With a groan he buried his head against them.

Bree swayed toward him, as caught up as he was now. She tightened her hands on his shoulders. In a frantic rush to feel the warmth of his skin against her fingertips, she tore at the buttons of his shirt.

They fell on the bed, still clothed, mouth pressed to mouth, whispering each other's names. With a groan Miguel sat up and pulled the black skirt and the sheer hose down over her hips. The high heels clattered on the terrazzo floor. He ripped his own clothes off and took her into his arms again.

Bree had almost forgotten—how *could* she have forgotten—the texture of his skin, his special scent, the feel of his arms around her as he pressed her closer. She lifted her body to his. She licked his shoulder, tasting him, and ran her hands up and down his back.

In a fever of desire she slid her hands over his hips, and lower, to touch the throbbing, virile heart of him.

Miguel groaned aloud. Then fearful that he might explode he crushed her to him and covered her body with his.

Bree looked up at him, lost and drowning in the darkness of his eyes, home at last in the shelter of his arms.

He thrust himself into her and Bree cried out her pleasure. She wanted to become a part of him, she wanted to lose herself in his embrace. His breath rasped against her throat and his hands went around her back to cradle her to him. His lips found hers in a kiss that shattered her with passion.

Bree caressed his shoulders, his sleekly muscled back, rained kisses on his face and throat and nuzzled her face against the thick mat of his chest hair as she strained closer.

He ground his mouth against hers. "Tell me you love me," he said against her lips.

"Oh, I do, Miguel. Yes, I love you."

Bree lifted her body to his. She wanted to give him everything—all of herself, everything she had, everything she was. She belonged to him, as he belonged to her.

When, in the back of her mind, she remembered that she would soon leave him, she began to weep. She dug her fingers into his shoulders and lifted her body to move frantically, desperately against him.

When it was over, when still her body trembled against his, Miguel held her close and kissed her, feeling the tears against his lips. "Darling," he said. "What is it?"

Bree clung to him, unable to speak as she burrowed closer.

A frown creased Miguel's forehead. He smoothed the fair hair back from her face and when at last she began to relax he asked, "What was it you wanted to tell me, Bree?"

"Not now," she said. "I'm so sleepy..." Her voice trailed off and she pretended to sleep. Tomorrow, she thought. I'll tell him tomorrow.

The morning dawned bright and clear with promise. Miguel awoke slowly. He stretched and reached for Bree. When he realized she wasn't beside him he opened his eyes. "Bree?" he said. He sat up and running a hand through his tousled hair looked around the room.

He saw her out on the balcony. She was dressed in one of his shirts, looking out toward the sea.

For a moment Miguel didn't move. He remembered the fear he'd felt when she said she had something to tell him. He remembered her tears.

Slowly, reluctantly, he got out of bed and pulled on a pair of jeans. He crossed the room to the French doors and went out to the balcony.

"What's the matter, love?"

"Nothing." Her voice was muffled. "I couldn't sleep."

Miguel put his hands on her shoulders and turned her to face him. "You're crying," he said. "What is it? What's troubling you, Bree?"

Not answering his question, Bree touched his face. She turned away and when her voice was under control she said, "I love your house, Miguel. It's beautiful. The view of the sea is breathtaking."

He wanted to insist she tell him what was wrong. But because he was afraid he said, "I have a surprise, something I've been wanting to tell you ever since you got off the plane."

Bree looked up at him. Her eyes, washed by the tears, were very clear and green. "What is it, Miguel?"

Miguel rested his hands on her waist. "I've outfitted the yawl for a cruise—she'll be ready by Sunday." He waited and when she didn't speak he said, "Two weeks, Bree. We'll have two weeks in the sun. We'll sail to Andros, Nassau, Eleuthera—wherever you'd like to go. Just the two of us, Bree. You can take your cameras and—"

"I can't." She looked at him, then away.

"What do you mean you can't?"

"I've got to go back to New York next week. Something's come up. I . . . I can't stay much longer, Miguel. I'm sorry."

"What has come up?" he asked quietly.

"I've been reassigned—I'm going to Rome."

"Rome?"

"It's a great opportunity." Her words came fast, tumbling over each other. "I'll be head of the office there. I can pick the assignments, go where I want to go, shoot what I want to shoot. But I . . . I have to be there as soon as I can. The man who's been in charge is leaving next month. I have to be there before then." She took a deep breath. "It's a great opportunity," she repeated.

"I see."

"We could take a short cruise," Bree said. "A couple of days. Maybe next summer—"

Miguel stepped away from her and shook his head. "No," he said. "No, not a short cruise now, not a two-week cruise next summer."

"Miguel, please—"

He shook his head. "No, Bree. I'm sorry, but no. A two-week affair isn't what I'm looking for."

She lifted her chin. "Then what are you looking for?"

"Commitment, Bree—a lifetime commitment. I want to marry you. I want to have children with you." A muscle in his jaw jumped as he tried to steady his voice. "I respect your work, Bree, and I know how important your profession is to you. I'm not asking you to give it up, I'm only asking that you do it here."

"In Key West?" she asked incredulously.

Miguel nodded. "Why not? You love the ocean, Bree. Nobody sees it the way you do. You could do a book about the sea. We'd sail down to the Caribbean, or across the Gulf to Mexico. I'd take time off from work. We could spend months at sea. We could—"

Bree stepped away from him. "I'm not that kind of a photographer, Miguel. I'm a photojournalist—I need news and events. The Rome office is just too good an opportunity to pass up." She struggled for words to make him understand. "I love you, Miguel. I want to be with you, but . . ." She turned away and fought for control. "Give me a year," she said. "Two years. I'll come back. I swear I'll come back."

"You want me to wait two years?" Miguel shook his head. "No, Bree," he said. "I love you—I'll always love you, but I can't do that." He looked at her, then turned to go inside. At the door he hesitated. "I set sail on Sunday," he said. "With you or without you."

When he disappeared into the room Bree stayed where she was. She looked out at the blue and endless sea through eyes blinded by tears. She knew that she'd lost him.

Chapter Fifteen

That afternoon Miguel drove Bree home, dressed again in the black suit and hat, looking as though she'd just arrived from Miami.

"I don't want to upset you," Miguel said before they got out of the car. "And I don't mean what I said to sound like an ultimatum, Bree, but I can't build my life on your comings and goings. If a man loves a woman—and make no mistake, I do love you—he wants to be with her all of the time. I don't want a part-time lover, I want a wife who wants to be with me as much as I want to be with her."

"I do love you, Miguel," Bree said. "But—"

"Yeah, it's that 'but' that's the problem, isn't it?" He started to get out of the car but Bree put a restraining hand on his arm.

Tears like small white diamonds shone in her eyes. "It's a hard decision to make," she said. "This promotion came up so fast. I need time to think. I need..." She shook her head, unable to go on. "I love you," she whispered.

Miguel looked at Bree for a long moment. "As I said, I'm leaving for the islands on Sunday morning," he said. "If you make up your mind by then what it is you want, you know where to find me."

He tightened his hands on the steering wheel, holding himself back because he wanted to drive away with her—to kidnap her and carry her aboard one of his boats like some black-bearded pirate of the 1700s. But this wasn't the 1700s and he wasn't a pirate. Bree was a free woman, with freedom of choice. The decision was hers to make.

Almost reluctantly Miguel got out of the pickup and carried her bags up to her mother's front porch. He wanted to kiss her but he was afraid if he did he wouldn't be able to stop at that. Instead of a kiss he rested a hand on her beautifully coiffed hair. "I like it better down," he said quietly, then turned and went back down the walk.

"You look tired," Cornelia said when she opened the door. "Come into the kitchen, I've made some tea. Was it a good flight today? Did you have to wait very long for your connection?"

"No, I..." Bree hesitated. Then unable to lie, she said, "I didn't come in today, mother. I came in yesterday."

"Oh?" Cornelia's eyebrows raised. "Where've you been? With Miguel?"

"Yes, I'm sorry. I should have called you."

"Yes, you should have." Cornelia poured the tea and brought the cups to the table. "You're a grown woman, Brianna Petersen. I can't tell you what to do.

You've never been flighty and I don't suppose you've started now. You *are* in love with Miguel aren't you?"

"Yes, mother, I'm in love with him."

"Has he asked you to marry him?"

"Yes."

"Well, thank goodness." Cornelia looked at Bree and seeing the distress on her daughter's face said, "Then what's the matter? You said yes, didn't you?"

Bree shook her head.

"Why ever not?"

She looked down at the cup of tea. "Mr. Henderson wants me to go to Rome."

"Rome!" Cornelia shook her head as though to clear it. "That's farther away than Paris!"

"Not much." Bree tried to smile, but the smile faded before it took shape. "It's a wonderful opportunity, Mother. I'd be in charge of the office. I could choose my own assignments, and follow up on whatever story interested me. You could come over. We could go to Venice—"

"I don't want to go to Venice." Cornelia glared at Bree. "What about Miguel?" she asked. "Is that the reason you won't marry him?"

Bree nodded, almost too upset by now to try to speak. But she wanted her mother to understand how she felt, so she said, "I tried to explain to him how important this promotion is to me. I asked him to give me some time. I'd try to come back here for Christmas, he could come to Rome for a week or two. We could work it out."

"Would you be married before you left?"

"No, that wouldn't work, it wouldn't be fair to either of us."

"But you'd expect him to wait around for you?"

Bree frowned. "I know that sounds difficult, but—"

"Difficult?" Cornelia gave an uncharacteristic snort. "It sounds impossible. No wonder Miguel refused."

"You don't understand." Bree averted her face. "I have a right to pursue my career. Miguel should understand that."

Cornelia pursed her lips in an expression Bree remembered all too well. She got up, and poured herself more tea. Before she could sit down the phone rang. She answered it and a smile softened her face. "I did, too," she said into the phone. "Tonight?" She glanced at Bree. "Yes, tonight would be fine. Seven o'clock? Yes, all right. I'll see you then.

"That was Antonio," Cornelia said when she sat down. "We're going to Louie's Backyard for dinner tonight. I haven't been there in years."

Bree stirred her tea. Glad to have the conversation turn away from her, she said, "Is everything still all right between the two of you?"

"Better than all right." Cornelia cleared her throat. She looked at Bree and hot color flooded her cheeks. "Antonio asked me to marry him last night," she said.

Almost too stunned to speak, Bree managed to say, "What did you . . . what was your answer?"

"I said yes, of course. We're going to be married some time next spring."

"Well, I . . ." Bree looked at her mother. "I don't know what to say." She felt the sting of tears behind her eyelids as she got up. Going to her mother she kissed her and said, "I'm so happy for you, Mother."

"Oh, Bree. I love Antonio and I want to spend the rest of my life with him." Cornelia put her arms around her daughter. "But I want you to be happy, too."

"I will be, Mother, one of these days when the timing's right." Then, because Bree was afraid she was going to cry, she went into the living room to get the box from Saks. "Maybe you'd like to wear this tonight," she said when she came back into the room.

Cornelia opened the box. With an exclamation of pleasure she held up the pale green dress. "Oh, isn't this the prettiest thing I've ever seen! I believe I *will* wear it tonight, Bree. Thank you."

"You're welcome. Would you like me to take it upstairs for you? I'm going to unpack."

And pack. Still stunned by her mother's announcement, Bree looked around her room, trying to decide what she would need to take with her to Italy. Most of her things were in Paris. She slumped down on the bed. She'd have to get rid of the Paris apartment, pack all of her things and send them on to Rome once she had an apartment there.

Bree leaned against the bedpost and watched the afternoon sun filter in through the open window to pattern the worn carpet. A faint breeze stirred the starched white curtains. She closed her eyes and breathed in the moist, warm air.

Soon the winter season would begin and the snowbirds from the north would come to bask in the temperate, sun-filled days. By summer, the heat and humidity would envelop the island like a hot, white tent. The tourists would leave and the Key Westers with enough money to get away would flock to the mountains of North Carolina. But the old-timers would stay because this was where they belonged.

But it wasn't where she belonged.

That night after her mother went out Bree went to the hospital to see Craig. He said that he was better and that Bobbie, who'd just left, was going to take him home the following day.

He took Bree's hand enthusiastically. "I did what you told me to do. A cardiologist came in today and examined me. The cardiogram was fine. He won't get the results of the blood workups for a day or so, but he's pretty sure I'm okay."

"I'm glad, Craig. And I'm so pleased that things are going well for you and Bobbie." She hesitated. "I'll be leaving in a few days."

"So soon? I must say, I'm really surprised, Bree. I could have sworn you and Miguel had something going. I thought maybe he'd talk you into staying."

Bree shook her head. Forcing a smile she said, "Nope, I'm afraid not. I'm heading for New York and then Rome."

"Rome?"

"Land of pasta, sunshine and the Trevi Fountain." Suddenly she really didn't want to talk about it. Kissing Craig's forehead she said, "Visiting hours are about over. You need your rest for that big move tomorrow. I'll be in touch before I leave."

It wasn't quite dark when Bree left the hospital. The evening was calm, the temperature in the seventies. She didn't want to go home so she went down to Duval Street, toward Mallory Square. She strolled for a long time, looking in shop windows, listening to the music coming from Sloppy Joe's and the other small bars along the street. Finally she went to the sunset deck of the Pier House and had a solitary drink overlooking the ocean.

Except for the murmur of voices and the occasional tourist who jumped up to take a picture of the sunset, it was quiet. Pelicans dozed on dock poles while sea gulls floated aloft or suddenly swooped low for a fish. Pleasure boats and fishing boats came into the bay from the sea while a guitarist sang quietly. The sky turned flamingo red and the clouds drifted close to the water like mountains of fluff painted by a punch-drunk artist. Splashes of gray turned the blue water dark, then darker. She wondered if a camera could ever capture the beauty before her.

Bree sat there until the last brilliant rays of the sun faded into the sea and night settled in. The sunset watchers and the tourists left. Only she and a guitarist and the pelicans remained.

The next day she went down to Mallory Square again and, like a tourist, rode the Conch Tour Train for a fourteen-mile tour of Key West. She listened to the story of old and new Key West, of the Spanish conquistadors, the pirates and the great wrecking days.

She said goodbye to the place she loved most in the world.

The yawl had been repainted. Her hull had been scraped, the cutlass bearing and the prop had been checked out and the rudder posts were in good shape.

Sweat ran down Miguel's tanned body as he checked the sails and adjusted the shrouds. The radio was in good working order and the galley was stocked with canned goods. There was a jug of rum in the bar and beer in the refrigerator. Tomorrow he'd buy steaks for the freezer and pick up enough fruit and vegetables to last until he got to Nassau.

He'd heard nothing from Bree—but there were three more days until Sunday.

Miguel wiped the sweat off his face with a clean white handkerchief and looked out over the water. His face was haggard and drawn and there were patches under his eyes, sad evidence of sleepless nights when he'd roamed his empty house and of dawns he'd spent out on the patio overlooking the sea, waiting for that first faint streak of sunlight on the horizon. Twice he'd almost called Bree. He'd even dialed the number once, but at the last minute he'd replaced the phone. He wouldn't beg. Whatever she decided had to be her decision.

But whatever the decision, on Sunday morning he would set sail.

The new issue of *Our World Magazine* came out Saturday morning. By noon everyone in town was talking about Bree's photographs.

Dawn called her immediately. "I've just seen the magazine. Your pictures are great. I knew you were good, but I had no idea *how* good."

Bobbie Lee called. She tried to tell Bree how good the photos were and burst into tears. When she stopped crying she told her that she and Craig were leaving for Jamaica in two weeks for a vacation.

Miguel's reaction was different from that of most of the people in Key West. He studied the pictures carefully, thoughtfully. They were good, so good he felt the short hairs rise on the back of his neck. They told the story of Hurricane Lola even better than Bree's eyewitness account of the storm. There was a poignancy to the photos that words could never describe. It was as though Bree had the ability of looking into the heart of the people she photographed and she made them come alive with feeling.

He turned back to the front cover, to the photo of the woman and the little girl scratching through the wreckage of their home. The woman looked directly into the camera with haunted, angry eyes. There was an expression on her face that seemed to say, "I've lost it all, how dare you take my pride?"

Miguel leaned back in a deck chair. How did Bree feel when she'd taken that shot? Did she weep for the woman and the little girl with the broken doll or did she look through the lens of her camera and see only how they would look on the front cover of a magazine?

Once again he looked through the ten pages of her photographs. The one of Captain Bob was a classic. The old man had already seen it and shown it to everyone within shouting distance.

But some of Bree's other shots—of an elderly couple weeping as they stared at all that remained of their home in Windley Key, of the ships that had smashed and gone aground, of the grieving wife of a fisherman who had been lost at sea—troubled him. For although the photographs were sensitive, it seemed to Miguel that Bree had separated herself from her subjects completely.

He knew that in the way a doctor couldn't get emotionally involved with a patient, a newsman or a photographer couldn't get involved in every story they were covering. A frown creased Miguel's forehead. Had he been right when he'd told Bree she was an outsider who only looked at life through the lens of her camera?

He'd told her that he thought photographing human tragedy was obscene. That was unfair and untrue. Bree had only been doing her job. She'd done it well—better, he thought, than anyone else could have. No wonder she'd been promoted to head the Rome office. She was good. She was damn good.

How could he expect her to give it all up to marry him?

In the late afternoon on Saturday Bree retreated to the attic room where she'd spent so many hours when she was young. There, on the padded seat in the dormer window, she looked down at the yard below. This was where she'd dreamed of all the things she would do when she grew up. She'd dreamed of Craig Logan and of being famous. She's dreamed of traveling the world.

It's funny, Bree thought now—she'd never dreamed of Miguel. Maybe that had been because Miguel had always been there. He was reality. The rest of it had been only an illusion. Miguel was all that was real in her life.

Bree reached in her canvas bag and pulled out the magazine. With a photographer's eye she studied the shot on the front cover. It was good—it was probably the best thing she'd ever done. Sun and shadow had been right, the composition was good. It was something she could be proud of. And yet . . .

Bree stared at the woman who stared back at her and something twisted in her heart—she knew she'd callously invaded this woman's privacy. She'd intruded on a very personal grief in a time of crisis and pain.

"But that's my job," she whispered. Wasn't that what she'd said to Miguel? She did her job and she did it well. Then why did she feel ashamed of this picture, of this woman who looked at her so accusingly?

Bree felt the sting of tears behind her eyelids. She reached into her purse for a tissue and saw the copy of *Peter Pan* she'd picked up in the bookstore in New York. She hadn't read the book since she was a child. She'd only bought it because of Miguel, because he'd told her he'd taken the name of his yawl from one of its passages.

Now she opened it and began to read the magical story of Peter, Wendy, Tinkerbell, and the children.

It was quiet in the secluded alcove at the top of the old Victorian house. The only sound was the brush of the branches of the Spanish laurel tree against the window.

Slowly Bree turned the pages of the book. It seemed to her, as she read, that she could almost see Miguel—or the boy he'd been—reading these very same words, his face wrinkled in concentration over the unfamiliar English.

She'd read somewhere that Mary Martin, the most famous Peter Pan of all, had once said, "Never Never Land is the way I would like real life to be—timeless, free, mischievous, filled with gaiety, tenderness and magic."

Filled with gaiety, tenderness and magic. What had those words meant to a young Cuban boy, a boy who'd left his friends behind in the land he would never return to?

Twilight settled over the attic room before Bree closed the book. She sat for a long time, looking out past the trees to the quiet street below. It seemed to her that somewhere in the distance she could smell the sea.

Chapter Sixteen

At six-thirty on Sunday morning Cornelia knocked on Bree's door. "I hope I didn't wake you," she said. "I thought you might like a cup of coffee."

Bree sat up and fluffed a pillow behind her back. "You didn't wake me."

"It's a beautiful day and since you're leaving tomorrow, I thought you might want to make the most of it." Cornelia glanced at Bree's suitcase. "I see you've almost finished packing. What time's your flight?"

"At ten." Bree avoided her mother's eyes as she reached for the coffee. "You're all dressed," she said. "Are you going to church?"

"No, I'll go later with Antonio. He's coming by for me in about an hour." Cornelia hesitated. "We're going to see Miguel off."

"Oh." Bree concentrated on her coffee. "He's...going to the islands, then?"

"Yes, it seems as though he is—with or without you."

"What time is he leaving?" she asked.

"Eight or so." Cornelia waited. "You're not going to see him off?"

Bree shook her head. "I have to finish packing."

When her mother didn't answer, Bree looked up. Cornelia's arms were folded across her chest and her lips were pursed disapprovingly.

"I have a lot to do, Mother," Bree said defensively.

Cornelia nodded. She started toward the door, hesitated and turned back. "We're a lot alike, you and I. I know you never thought so, but we are. It's hard for us to turn our backs on a way of life we've been accustomed to, even though that life might not be all it was cracked up to be. We're afraid of change, even when the change might give us everything we've ever dreamed of." She took a step toward Bree and her voice softened when she said, "It's hard to put your life in someone else's hands, to rely on them for your warmth and your happiness—to give yourself up completely. I've never been able to do that, Bree." Cornelia cleared her throat. "Until now."

"But Daddy..." Bree stared at her mother. "You were married a long time, you loved each other."

"I loved him as much as I was capable of loving then, but I never was able to give...all of myself. There was always a part of me that I held in reserve." Cornelia's voice quavered. "But I'm learning, Bree, because Antonio is teaching me. I'm finding out that to be completely loved, you must completely love. You have to give, and that's been a hard lesson for me to learn." The shadow of a smile crossed Cornelia's face. "But my, what joy there is in the learning, Bree."

The silence of the room was broken by the softly plaintive call of a dove. Cornelia looked at her daughter's bent head. Bree's face was hidden beneath her hair, but Cornelia knew that she was crying.

She touched the top of her daughter's head. "I made some blueberry muffins for your breakfast," she said. "I've invited Antonio and Lupita to have dinner with us later. We'll eat about five if that's all right with you."

"That's fine," Bree said softly.

Her mother went out and closed the door, leaving her alone. Bree hunched over, head against her knees, and let the tears come.

Outside the dove called again to its mate.

Bree stayed like she was for a long time. In a little while she heard a car drive up, then the front door open and close.

When she knew that she was alone she got out of bed. She took a shower and washed her hair, and when she came out of the bathroom, her eyes still red from weeping, she began putting things in her suitcase.

She picked up the copy of *Peter Pan* from the nightstand. She stood, there in the quiet of the room, and held it to her breast.

The sun was bright and the wind was up. It was a day meant for sailing. Miguel stood on the deck of *Straight On Till Morning* with his father and Cornelia.

"Where're you heading first?" Antonio asked.

"Andros," Miguel said. "I'll put in for fresh supplies before I go on to Nassau. I might spend a day or two there. If the weather's good and I've got the time I'll go on to Eleuthera." He looked at his father. "I feel guilty about leaving you with everything, but I really need to get away for a while."

"Sure you do." Antonio put his arm around his son's shoulders. "When you come back maybe I'll take a little vacation." He grinned at Cornelia, who blushed and pretended to be interested in a swooping gull. "I've got a friend who's never been to St. Croix. I've been telling her all about it and I'm trying to get her to fly over there with me."

"Good luck," Miguel said with a smile. But something twisted inside him at the irony of the situation—Cornelia and his father together, while he and Bree were apart. He glanced at his watch, then looked down the dock toward the street that led to the marina.

"It's almost eight-thirty," he said. "The wind's good now, I guess it's about time to shove off. Tell Lupita I'll bring her a bottle of perfume from Nassau."

Antonio embraced his son. *"Vaya con Dios,"* he said.

"Thank you, Dad." Miguel took Cornelia's hand. "Tell Bree—" he paused in mid-sentence. There wasn't anything to tell Bree. Once more he raised he eyes to the end of the dock. The empty dock.

"I'm sorry," Cornelia said.

"So am I." Miguel kissed her cheek and helped her out of the boat.

His father untied the mooring rope and handed it down to him. "Call me from Andros," he said.

"I will." Miguel raised the anchors, then lifted his hand for a final goodbye as he cast off. The sails furled and grabbed the wind. He turned away just as Antonio shouted, ''Wait!''

He looked back as a taxi screeched to a stop at the end of the dock. A figure, blond hair blowing in the wind, leapt out. She waved and shouted, ''Wait for me!''

Miguel's breath caught in his throat as Bree sprinted down the dock. She was dressed in shorts and a T-shirt. She had a duffle bag over her shoulder.

As Miguel eased the boat back toward the dock she ran toward him. ''Permission to come aboard, sir,'' she said tremulously.

Miguel looked up at her. ''This is a lifetime cruise,'' he said. ''The boat doesn't stop in Rome.''

''I don't want to go to Rome.''

''Bree...'' He took a breath to steady himself. ''Are you sure?''

''Surer than I've ever been in my life.'' She held her hand out to him. ''If you still want me,'' she said.

''I want you.'' Miguel's voice was hoarse with emotion. He took her hand. ''Permission granted,'' he said and brought her down into his arms.

Bree clung to him and when he let her go she saw that his eyes were filled with tears. ''It's the sun,'' he said, then laughed and hugged her. ''All ready to go?''

''Yes.'' She held her hands up to her mother and Antonio. ''I left Alex's number next to the phone,'' she told her mother. ''Will you call him tomorrow? Tell him I'm sorry. Tell him Rome sounds wonderful but that I've had a better offer.'' She felt Miguel tighten his hand on hers. ''And Mother, if you have time, you might begin to plan a wedding for some time next month." Bree looked at Miguel. "Maybe Thanksgiving?"

"Thanksgiving's fine," he said.

Cornelia laughed and waved as a puff of breeze caught the sails, billowing them full and white against the blue sky.

Miguel, his hand gentle on the tiller, headed out toward the deep turquoise water. He put his arm around Bree and drew her closer. "I love you," he said. "I don't know what made you decide to come with me, but I thank God that you did."

That night at dusk they anchored near a small island, and while Bree went below to prepare their supper, Miguel made two cool drinks and brought them up to the deck where he placed thick mats and pillows side by side so they could sit and watch the sunset.

When Bree came up, he gave her one of the glasses and they sat together without speaking as the sky turned from blue shot with glorious shades of red, to dusty pink and finally to gold.

The boat rocked gently beneath them and as the sky darkened Miguel put his arms around Bree and kissed her. "I love you," he murmured against her lip. "You know that, don't you?"

"Yes, Miguel." Bree kissed him. "Yes, darling, I know."

Miguel gathered her in his arms. Bree, his Bree, the sweet promise of all his dreams come true at last.

For a long time they didn't speak. One by one the stars began to appear. Bree leaned back in Miguel's arms, happier than she'd ever been in her life. She looked up at the sky. "Which star is it?" she asked.

Miguel raised his arm and pointed. "Second star on the right," he said. "Straight on till morning."

*   *   *   *   *

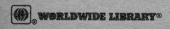

Silhouette Intimate Moments

NEXT MONTH
CHECK IN TO
DODD MEMORIAL HOSPITAL!

Not feeling sick, you say? That's all right, because Dodd Memorial isn't your average hospital. At Dodd Memorial you don't need to be a patient—or even a doctor yourself!—to examine the private lives of the doctors and nurses who spend as much time healing broken hearts as they do healing broken bones.

In UNDER SUSPICION (Intimate Moments #229) intern Allison Schuyler and Chief Resident Cruz Gallego strike sparks from the moment they meet, but they end up with a lot more than love on their minds when someone starts stealing drugs—and Allison becomes the main suspect.

In May look for AFTER MIDNIGHT (Intimate Moments #237) and finish the trilogy in July with HEARTBEATS (Intimate Moments #245).

Author Lucy Hamilton is a former medical librarian whose husband is a doctor. Let her check you in to Dodd Memorial—you won't want to check out!

IM229-1

Silhouette Romance™
Legendary Lovers Trilogy

BY DEBBIE MACOMBER....

ONCE UPON A TIME, in a land not so far away, there lived a girl, Debbie Macomber, who grew up dreaming of castles, white knights and princes on fiery steeds. Her family was an ordinary one with a mother and father and one wicked brother, who sold copies of her diary to all the boys in her junior high class.

One day, when Debbie was only nineteen, a handsome electrician drove by in a shiny black convertible. Now Debbie knew a prince when she saw one, and before long they lived in a two-bedroom cottage surrounded by a white picket fence.

As often happens when a damsel fair meets her prince charming, children followed, and soon the two-bedroom cottage became a four-bedroom castle. The kingdom flourished and prospered, and between soccer games and car pools, ballet classes and clarinet lessons, Debbie thought about love and enchantment and the magic of romance.

One day Debbie said, "What this country needs is a good fairy tale." She remembered how well her diary had sold and she dreamed again of castles, white knights and princes on fiery steeds. And so the stories of Cinderella, Beauty and the Beast, and Snow White were reborn....

Look for Debbie Macomber's *Legendary Lovers* trilogy from Silhouette Romance: *Cindy and the Prince* (January, 1988); *Some Kind of Wonderful* (March, 1988); *Almost Paradise* (May, 1988). Don't miss them!

SRT-1